Beethoven's Tenth

In post-Napoleonic Europe, rival secret societies hunt for Beethoven's Tenth Symphony—for whomever deciphers the intricate mathematics hidden within, gains power over time and space.

Trestan Descaix, Napoleon's best spy, seeks the Tenth's hidden transcripts for Revolutionary partisans. The quest will send him across time, braving horrors from Borodino to Auschwitz, and ultimately to other worlds in a race to decide the course of humanity. Composers living and dead aid or hinder his efforts. Yet a mysterious competitor not only challenges him for the Tenth, but challenges the Enlightenment ideals he's claimed to uphold—and his betrayals in doing so.

BEETHOVEN'S TENTH

TONY PEAK

Acknowledgment

Thanks to my agent Ethan Ellenberg for providing this opportunity for Beethoven's Tenth to see publication. To Ian Welke, Kim Heniadis, and Gregory Clifford for their critiques. And to my family for their support in those moments when all I heard was dirges rather than symphonies.

Table of Contents

MOVEMENT I

1.

Overture in D minor, Opus 31
March 29th, 1827
Vienna

Trestan sprinted across the dunes, but the figure far outdistanced him. Music echoed behind him, music not performed by human hand. The vibrations emanating from it made him stumble in the sand.

He would not reach the columns in time.

The Broadwood's strings warbled and popped as flames devoured the piano. Each tightly bound metal wire, exposed like the sinews of an industrial beast, snapped apart in a staccato volley. The noise's brusque atonality made Trestan jump. No matter how hard he tried forgetting, the sounds of war, of death, were ever fresh memories.

Embers suffused the air as the fire spread throughout the apartment. Voices echoed in the street below. Though the occupant had been buried earlier, Trestan gripped the pistol inside his waistcoat. The creak of weakened beams made him hurry.

He passed a stack of blackened, curling manuscripts, victims of the rising heat. Tuning pins and key levers popped from a burning harpsicord. A hissing noise made Trestan turn. It was a brass ear trumpet, melting in the flames. Nothing was spared in the House of the Black-Robed Spaniards, Beethoven's final home.

Trestan hurried to a bookshelf and yanked out volume after volume, seeking anything written in the late composer's scrawl. The books were hot to the touch. Sweat stung Trestan's eyes, smoke stole his breath. Something must be here, else the bastards would not have set the residence aflame. Their fabricated Hell would not stop him.

The tuning fork in his jacket vibrated. Trestan pressed a hand against it, fearing it might leap from his pocket. He'd never used one before. The technology his superiors used was strange, but it had transported him here. He hoped it transported him out.

The vibration repeated, audible this time: a slight pulsation singing through the air, a delicate fingernail tapping a wound copper wire. Trestan ignored the books and concentrated on the sound, the tuning fork directing him. He ducked through a burning doorway into Beethoven's sitting room. Wallpaper curled off the walls like leprotic flesh, pocked with flaming holes. They reminded him of the dead at Valencia, at Salamanca. Piled corpses ready for Moloch's altar. Reminding him of those he'd betrayed.

He threw aside a sedan chair and snatched up the vibration's source.

It was another tuning fork, lying in a pool of blood. The crimson mirror reflected the growing inferno around Trestan. Damnation was never patient.

He lifted the fork, which quivered despite his vengeful grip. It was a semi-tone higher than his, piercing his eardrum. Gritting his teeth, Trestan pressed hands over ears to stave off the aural assault. But the semi-tone rang throughout the apartment, a final note in Beethoven's dirge.

The vibration ended abruptly. Some ceiling collapsed, blocking the doorway with burning timbers. Cinders zipped through the air, incinerating hundreds of holes into Trestan's clothing. He patted them out and shoved the fork into his pocket.

The building shook as more ceiling surrendered to the con-flagration. Trestan held a handkerchief to his mouth, coughing as smoke stole reality. His boots crunched through a fallen vase, his knees scraped past the ironically dead furnace. Something snapped underfoot, and he glimpsed a black mask through the smoke. A gaunt, knowing visage, come to claim him from an earthly inferno for the one surely awaiting him after death.

It had Beethoven's face.

Windows shattered, and the influx of oxygen fed the starving blaze. Trestan fell prone as a cascade of angry flame whooshed over his head. The entire building groaned under the hellish assault. Trestan dared not breathe, knowing it would be his last. His hand scrabbled over scorched tiles until his fingers closed around the mask's remnants. Only then did he flee, on all fours like a hellhound from the kennels of Hades.

The fire roared above him, and Trestan bit his tongue against touching the hot floor. Still he crawled, until he reached another window. He rolled aside and kicked the lower windowsill. The burned, damaged wood gave way to his crushing heels. Heated splinters stung him as Trestan thrust from the makeshift portal.

He hit the debris-strewn sidewalk, then fled until his boots scraped over cobblestones. Lowering the handkerchief, he sucked in deep, hungry breaths. With the heat no longer threatening him, Trestan turned.

Beethoven's apartment fell in upon itself amidst clouds of embers and ash. Flaming timbers thudded onto the street. The piano's lower-key bass strings popped like a cannonade, echoing through Vienna. A mocking salute to Trestan's failure.

He removed his hat, wiped his brow, then remembered he still held the mask. The eyeholes and mouth were stark against the fire-lit night, an ebony countenance from the abyss. Other than the bloodied tuning fork, it was the only thing he'd found. Beethoven's Tenth Symphony might be ashes now, since Trestan had not discovered it.

The only explanation was that someone knew he would be coming.

He slid the mask into his jacket and staggered from the humorless pyre. Fresh snow fell, though it melted whenever it landed on Trestan. He still radiated heat. But unlike Orpheus entering Hell, he was none the wiser. Nothing to report but the arson, the mask, and that damnable tuning fork.

"Halt!" someone shouted in German.

"Yes, what is it?" Trestan asked, affecting his best Viennese gentlemen's accent.

Figures in coats and bicorne hats crept toward him. Though the oil lamps lining the thoroughfares provided illumination, they didn't reveal the figures' identities.

"Stop where you are," another voice said. "Search him."

They seemed unconcerned that the home of Vienna's greatest composer was now a pile of cinders. It was safe to assume they were not of the fire brigade.

Safe to assume they already had pistols aimed at him beneath those dark jackets.

In all his years as Talleyrand's spy, for Napoleon, and then *Armée de L'ombre*, Trestan always trusted such instincts. They had never failed him. Even when the Allies marched through Paris after Waterloo, he knew when to blend in, when to flee.

Trestan raised his arms slowly, well away from the pistol in his waistcoat—but within reach of his chest pocket. As one of the figures came closer, Trestan bumped the back of his hand against the tuning fork in the chest pocket. The device vibrated.

"You stupid Frenchman," one of the figures muttered. "Think the Chorale's secrets will get you out of this? What did you find in Herr Beethoven's home?"

"This." Trestan whistled the closing notes of Beethoven's Fifth Symphony, a collection of C major notes, fortissimo. The tuning fork vibrated louder, deeper.

The figures drew pistols.

Marmont straightened in his saddle and smiled at the dust cloud ahead. "You did not lie, Monsieur Desaix. The British will never know what hit them."

Trestan offered his best smile. The same he used to fool enemy spies.

The next instant, Trestan stood ten feet away. His muscles quivered with fatigue, and he lost his breath. The device worked, just as Talleyrand said it would. But he wasn't sure if he stood in Vienna, or upon the arid Spanish plain with Marshal Marmont, fifteen years ago. He swayed, grasping for his horse in Spain, a street lamp in Vienna.

Trestan occupied both places, and yet neither.

Finally taking a breath, he forced himself down an adjacent alley. The tuning fork gave Trestan a full five seconds before his pursuers realized he'd fled, and gave chase.

Shouts sounded through the gloom. Sleepy citizens peeked out doors. Candles and lamps lit once-darkened windows as Trestan ran down street after street. He coughed and tasted ash. He'd breathed more smoke than he'd thought. The heavy jacket weighed him down. His boots screeched over the snow-moistened cobblestones.

Footsteps sounded in a nearby alley. Trestan flattened against a wall. The steps were amateurish, the movement of one who thought his passage was muted. That was another thing *Armée de L'ombre* had taught him—how to listen.

Trestan gripped his pistol. The steps came closer, around the corner.

He dared not use the tuning fork again. The previous use would have alerted any practitioners of metaphonics in the city; another attempt would lead them right to him.

A click sounded. A thumb pressing down a pistol hammer? The release of a blade from its sheath? Trestan remained still. Melted snow weighed his jacket.

Marshall Marmont grunted in agony as the physicians tried binding his broken ribs. Blood covered the stretcher he lay on, the larger red droplets shaken by each distant eruption of cannon fire. His arm lay at a twisted angle, and the old French surgeon tried to set it, but Marmont made sure to keep Trestan in his hateful gaze.

"You said Wellington sent Pakenham's division to reinforce the city!" Marmont reached after Trestan with his good arm, as if he could wring the truth from him.

"The British surprised us, sir." Trestan kept his hand near the pistol in his waistcoat. Though he wanted to turn the pistol on himself, rather than Marmont or his soldiers. Each time the cannons shook the earth, Trestan was reminded he'd betrayed his countrymen. Reminded that the

shell and shot cleaving apart French bodies was his doing. But he was sworn to this course. Sworn over the corpses of Spanish men, women, and children, victims of French liberation. His own countrymen, defiling the Revolution.

Marmont cursed him, but the physicians forced him to lie back, while the Count of Bonet galloped away with his staff, disappearing in a cloud of cannon smoke shortly after. Trestan remained still as the French lines charged, and he remained still while the stretcher bearers collected the wounded after Wellington had stomped the Imperial standard into the dirt. Eagles with shattered wings.

"Quintilius Varus, give me back my legions," Trestan whispered.

It was all his doing. A traitor to his emperor, to his country.

A figure rounded the corner, and the gleam of lamplight on metal told the story. Trestan had a clear shot; the bullet would crush the man's skull, though the sound and flash would give away Trestan's position. He hadn't killed a man in three years.

But the figure around the corner wasn't a man.

He glimpsed a metal face. Eyes like pools of darkness, and the mouth, a mere slot. Underneath its coat, the glimmer of breastplate. A chevalier of death.

A yellow flash struck the metal face, and the thing stumbled backward.

Trestan darted into the street, boots crunching through the snow. The flakes grew fatter and fell heavier. By the time he reached the exit point given him by Talleyrand, Trestan fled across a Teutonic glacier. He cocked the pistol's hammer, but kept it under his jacket to spare the powder from the elements.

Like any spy, he had one shot. It wasn't meant for his enemies.

Three times Trestan slipped on the city's numerous bridges. Vienna allegedly possessed four times as many as Venice. Trestan sought only one. Desperate breaths wafted from his lips, terminating in vaporous frost.

The exit point was a stone bridge near the city's outskirts. A carriage waited for him there, driven by the best horses this side of the Rhine. Trestan ran faster.

Something whizzed past his shoulder as the report of guns reached his ears. Another bullet tore through his sleeve, right above the skin. He tossed the jacket.

A figure stood in his path to the bridge. Metal face. Aiming a pistol.

The bullet smacked into a brick corner as Trestan ducked. He returned fire, then made straight for the bridge. His empty pistol clattered across rime-laden cobblestones.

Three years since he'd killed a man. Fifteen since he'd killed thirteen thousand.

The carriage horses neighed. More footsteps scraped behind him. The glow from the arson remained visible over Vienna's horizon, now reflected off a million snowflakes. Angel's tears for the last rites of the great Beethoven. The man whose music had helped defeat Napoleon. Another traitor to the Revolution, like Trestan.

The carriage door opened. An old but firm hand yanked Trestan inside. The door shut, and the horses cantered off the bridge. Down the street, several figures watched their egress with unblinking stares.

Trestan inhaled until his lungs hurt. His limbs quaked from the madcap marathon. Still clutching the damaged mask, still in possession of the bloodied tuning fork. The man opposite him could have been wearing a mask, for the dour, calculating frown was all anyone beheld on the face of Joseph Fouché, Napoleon's former Minister of Police.

"You were unsuccessful." Fouché always knew the outcome, condemning failures and stealing triumphs with but a glance.

Fixing his stare on the vista outside the carriage window, Trestan nodded. The Austrian countryside was a thicket of nightmares at such a late hour. It was more than the terrified observations of a nychtophobe, fearing the dark; the metal faces haunted his thoughts. Like toy lead soldiers enlarged and given life. Like the dead at Salamanca.

"Talleyrand doesn't have the infinite resources of the old Empire," Fouché said in his calm monotone. The same monotone that had unraveled Robespierre, the same monotone that had driven fear into Napoleon's heart. A dabbler in politics and intrigue since the Revolution, Fouché had mentored Trestan. Taught him when to lie, when to kill. Now, Fouché had been dead for seven years. A corpse out of time.

"Someone does." Trestan handed over the bloodied tuning fork and the black, damaged mask. Fouché examined them for a moment, then regarded Trestan like a rebellious dog who refused to perform tricks.

"*Armée de L'ombre* has many enemies." Fouché leaned forward, tapping the mask. "You may have created more."

Trestan allowed anger into his voice. "They knew I was coming. This was a trap."

Fouché's eyebrows rose. "Of course it was. You sprung it, but without any gains. Still, it might not all have been in vain. You acquired these items."

Trestan wondered if the old bastard would have saved him if he'd been caught in said trap. So he and Talleyrand had expected Trestan to fail. Years ago, such things wouldn't have bothered him. Before the massacres in Spain, he'd believed in the Revolution. Joined the military on his eighteenth birthday, after Napoleon's victory at Austerlitz. He'd never been prouder to be a Frenchman.

Now, because of the power Beethoven discovered and mastered, Napoleon had been defeated, the monarchy was ascendant, and the Revolution was but a memory.

"Yes. These items." Trestan shivered and accepted the new jacket Fouché offered him. "Where is Talleyrand?"

Fouché gave a thin, humorless smile and produced his own tuning fork. "We will go to him. Normal travel will be blocked from Austria, and our allies in Bohemia were compromised two days ago, omitting that route. Let our enemies find an empty carriage."

The fork shook in Fouché's hand, and ripples of force lapped against Trestan's body, his mind. His consciousness.

His back to the audience, Beethoven conducted the piece out of time. Yet the sound engulfed Trestan all the same, and he reached for her as the chorus joined in.

Trestan lowered his hands, but the music still rang in his ears.

"You have been eschewing the mental exercises I taught you." Fouché sniffed.

"No, I …" *He searched for her among the adoring crowd, but she was gone.*

With each ripple, time slowed, until the carriage halted, the horses froze in place, and the falling snow hung in midair. By the time Trestan realized what was happening, he stood in the vestibule of a great mansion. Wondering who he'd searched for.

Fouché opened a set of double doors. "He's been waiting for you."

2.

Adagietto in E major, Opus 31
March 29th, 1827
Château de Valençay

It took Trestan a moment to recognize the interior of Château de Valençay. Its Imperial stylings, extant in the form of carpeted tabourets, gilded tables shouldered by lions, and pavilion-like drapery, hearkened back to the Empire's glory days. Trestan felt a nostalgic sting of patriotism, tainted with guilt and time.

Those feelings quickly faded, since Fouché watched his every move as they entered the home of Charles Maurice de Talleyrand-Périgord. Château de Valençay had been in Talleyrand's possession since Imperial days, and Trestan had attended many parties there, spying on visiting foreign delegations. But the halls were silent now, and even Trestan's experienced eye couldn't discern any sentries.

A maid appeared, bidding them follow. Her pretty face labored to keep up a smile; Talleyrand rarely hired men for his spacious abode. As they passed through the halls, Trestan eyed the crystal chandeliers and oil paintings, ill-gotten through years of deceitful diplomacy and convenient, natural deaths. How Voltaire would have delighted at, and hated, such displays.

"You are fortunate, that you can still take to the field," Fouché said in a low voice. "Else you would have to serve *Armée de L'ombre* from these velvet catacombs."

"Fortunate?" Trestan frowned. "How many agents remain?"

"Thanks to his lack of foresight, you are now the last," Fouché said.

Trestan knew Fouché had once been Talleyrand's rival. Were it not for *Armée de L'ombre* going back in time and inducting him into their ranks, he supposed Fouché would rather remain dead.

The Shadow Army. That was what his order called itself. He'd joined two years after Waterloo, to restore France's former glory. Too desperate to be frightened by their strange devices, and now, too proud to enter domestic life, he was their foot soldier.

They entered Talleyrand's living room, a large chamber lit by several candelabras instead of oil lamps. Dozens of tiny, flickering suns flared for an instant, consuming the fresh oxygen ushered in by the maid. Another maid hurried out, cheeks flushed, eyes downcast. She slipped on the shoulder straps of her dress.

Talleyrand, wearing a blonde wig, supped from a goblet. His impeccable garments bordered on the aristocratic, which was once again the fashion. His very body language was a command, and his silence, an expectation.

"Fouché, you really should try some of this wine. Why, it will wrestle with your palate until you swear allegiance to its superior flavor." Talleyrand took another drink, swishing the liquid before swallowing.

"I cannot imagine your silver tongue swearing allegiance to anyone, *prince de Bénévent*," Fouché said without a trace of mockery. It was a call back to when Talleyrand had served the Empire. A reminder they had both betrayed Napoleon.

Talleyrand smiled, unoffended in the slightest. "Trestan, would you care for a drink? It is shameful to keep such treasures to oneself. Much like the thing you seek." Talleyrand waited as the maid refilled his cup, studying her beauty. Trestan knew better, and sensed the slight scolding inherent in Talleyrand's statement. It had taken him months to pick up on it, and he doubted if, even now, he knew how to interpret Talleyrand fully. Words were these men's weapon.

"I failed to discover any traces of Beethoven's last work, sir," Trestan said. "Someone set fire to the home before I arrived, and I barely escaped with my life."

Talleyrand fondled the maid's curly dark hair and shooed her away. "Hmm?" He watched her leave with the discerning eye of an old, shameless voluptuary, thinking his pornography an art rather than a vice.

Trestan looked away. The Revolution had died here long ago.

"He did escape with these tokens of daring." Fouché produced the tuning fork and mask, but his scorn made Trestan seethe with anger.

With shrewd eyes, Talleyrand examined the items. He gulped the wine, an effete Dionysus savoring the vitae of martyrs. "Ah. Our Teutonic rivals are at it again. How clever of them to fashion a new batch of these, after you allegedly destroyed that laboratory in Dresden, Fouché. So now the Russians and the Germans possess time travel. But even dead men make mistakes."

Fouché bristled like a starving dog whose food had been eaten in front of him. "They outnumber us…sir. Find me more trustworthy men, and I will deliver success."

Ignoring Fouché, Talleyrand ran bejeweled fingers over the mask. "They are as determined as they are brutish. But we require more proof, don't we, Trestan?"

It wasn't a question, but a command. Small wonder the old philanderer had outsmarted Napoleon, Tsar Alexander, Fouché, and others. It was such a mind that could lead them to what they needed. Let the aged fool have his courtesans and Beaujolais. Trestan would bring back the Revolution.

"It is Beethoven's face," Trestan said. "Found in his apartment."

"What else did you see?" Talleyrand studied Trestan.

"I encountered foes with metal faces," Trestan said. "Foes who did not bleed."

"I shot one in the face," Fouché said. "Though if Trestan had ran faster…"

Talleyrand scowled. "We have waited too long. Trestan's ignorance must be alleviated tonight, then. There is nothing else for it."

Fouché blanched, if it were possible for one so pale to lose even more color.

"I deserve to know," Trestan said. "I have proved my loyalty, my worth. I have spied, stolen, and killed for our cause. Yet France is no closer to freedom."

Their impenetrable host led them into a parlor containing two pianos, a harpsichord, and seats for a small musical ensemble. Violins, violas, piccolos, flutes, trumpets—some shone with new polish, while others were worm-ridden, or even burnt.

"Know you of the Chorale?" Talleyrand tapped a piano key with indifference.

"I'd heard they were a secret society of music enthusiasts," Trestan said.

"The Chorale discovered the science of metaphonics almost a century ago," Talleyrand said. "The early masters, such as Vivaldi, perfected mathematical formulas into their compositions. Formulas that harness the powers of the universe. In time, other master composers followed suit, and the Chorale's power grew. By the time Haydn took control of it, he had written many symphonies. He wrote many more afterward."

Trestan held up his tuning fork. "So a mere note grants one such witchery?"

"There are no such thing as witches," Talleyrand said. "Only the fools who fear them. The Chorale learned that their music could affect time and space. I realize that sounds worse than Voltaire or some other middle class philosopher, but it is true. These powers turned the war in their favor, defeating our emperor."

Fouché sniffed. "My men infiltrated the organization. We discovered their devices, and soon, we learned their use. Some of their number came over to us willingly. Others, less so. Tsar Alexander's Special Chancellery captured the rest."

"I thought Beethoven once admired the emperor?" Trestan asked.

Talleyrand smiled as if describing thunderclouds to a child. "After the emperor's coronation—where Napoleon took control of his own destiny and crowned himself—Beethoven, and many other 'artists', ceased their support. They wanted the rebellion of the poor, the ignorant, the laborers who cannot even spell their own name. No, for the Revolution to succeed, it must have a leader. One who is a revolution himself."

"Yet, that wasn't Napoleon." Fouché stabbed a discordant note on the piano.

"Then who?" Trestan eyed both men.

"Not who … but what." Talleyrand left the sitting room and walked out into the gardens. Two peacocks strode by, their rainbow plumage muted by the moonlight.

"Our enemies must have more information than we do," Trestan said. "They are ahead of us, since Beethoven's home offered no clues."

Talleyrand laughed. "None, you say?"

"The mask …?" Trestan's brow furrowed.

"You see, Fouché? He shows promise." Talleyrand clapped Trestan on the shoulder. "Indeed, the mask. Look at the lines along the facial features, the downcast countenance, the emaciated jowls … this is the face of a dead man."

Trestan unconsciously flicked his gaze at Fouché; the old man was staring right at him. "Beethoven's death mask."

"Indeed." Talleyrand handed the mask back to Trestan. "Our enemies wish to intimidate us. Like a Frenchman has never looked death in the face before."

Talleyrand and Fouché shared a spiteful glance.

"I know all about death." Trestan touched the mask's contours. A sad, hardened face. The visage of one who is frustrated that the rest of the world can't understand him.

"No … you do not." Fouché glowered at Talleyrand, then left the room.

Talleyrand gave a slight smile. "He despises me for bringing him to a future where he is already dead. It is his punishment for aiding in the execution of Marshal Ney. We could use the talents, the courage, of such men."

"You went back in time and acquired Fouché." Trestan left the question hanging.

"Our enemies have ways…" Talleyrand took a deep breath, and some of his age showed through his calm arrogance. "They have ways of misleading us through time. Beethoven's work gave power to all of us, but none will ever become ascendant until the Tenth is restored and its composition performed."

Trestan held up the mask to the moon, a half-phantom he would not fear. "Then I will uncover different ways, sir. I will see this through, on my word as a Frenchman."

Talleyrand held up his hands. "Ah, youth. It may save us yet. Come with me."

They reentered the mansion as Talleyrand struck a chime he'd produced from within his waistcoat. The tone vibrated, carrying across the lawn and into the house. Inside, Trestan stepped into a scene from years past. The Château was filled with dignitaries and soldiers from across the Empire. Officers in medal-laden uniforms, drank wine and laughed at hearty, adolescent jokes. Ladies in tight gowns fawned over these would-be Hannibals and Pompeys, but there was only one Caesar, and even he entertained a cadre of guests. A beauteous diva sang an aria from Paisiello's *Proserpine*.

Trestan now wore his old uniform, with furred pelisse over one shoulder, saber at his belt, and a white coatee over a navy blue jacket. Pride swelled his chest.

"Time is accessible via Beethoven's music," Talleyrand said, not caring if others overheard. "No other Chorale composer achieved that. Some managed to find other places out of a fairy tale, while some enhanced their bodies and minds with the vibrations of the universe. Yet, our enemies made all that you see here come to an end, when the Empire crumbled at the mercy of the music of the spheres."

A waiter brought them wine-filled glasses. Trestan brought it to his lips, but Talleyrand stopped him.

"Be wary of what you select as your addiction. This vice knows no return." Talleyrand nodded at the room, his expression grave. Like he'd seen all of these men and women die, and could not tell them. "Cheating time is a drug all its own, and a harsher master than any opiate. The Chorale knew this, and hid it from weaker minds."

"I will not fail." He met Talleyrand's eye and finished the wine in one gulp.

The guests burst into laughter, and Napoleon waved Talleyrand over. Merriment and spilled wine should have eased Trestan's decision, but he dashed his empty glass into a fireplace and walked back outside. He could control himself. Duty was his vice.

The other people vanished. He was back in his original clothing. Château de Valençay was quiet once more. A tomb, for all that had made it live was now gone.

Talleyrand joined him in the garden, the chime in his hand ceasing its vibration. "We need to find the other fragments of the Tenth Symphony. Follow our enemies' footsteps. That will lead you to the treasure of a deaf, angry man."

"I will seek out the sculptor of Beethoven's death mask." Trestan straightened. "But I shall like to make use of the bloodied tuning fork."

Narrowing his eyes, Talleyrand slowly handed it over. "Whatever for? Our own devices work just as well. Two forks might confuse the vibration, disrupt the energies."

"Whoever left this, either did so out of accident, or as a lure. I'll use it from now on." The dried blood was like thick lacquer, the red of a lady's nails. Trestan pocketed it, the action initiating a slight pulse.

Trestan raced across the dunes, but the figure was far ahead of him. He would not reach the columns in time. Music played somewhere behind him, music not performed by human hand. The vibrations made him stumble in the sand.

Trestan clasped his broken sword and continued toward the columns. He was a Mameluke charging the French at the Pyramids, he was a corsair on the Barbary Coast, he was a Gaul assaulting Alesia in vain. The sand grains had all been him over the eons, representing each time he'd made for those damned columns, how close he always came to completing the chase and finding—

"No return," Talleyrand said, watching him back on the Château grounds. "If you become trapped, there is no hope. Not even through time. Remember that."

Within the Château, a pianist played the opening notes to Beethoven's Ninth Symphony. The sound vibrated his tuning fork, and Trestan was no longer there.

3.

Fugato Lento in A minor, Opus 31
March 28th, 1827
Vienna

A lantern burned inside the studio, its dirty shade creating macabre silhouettes. Paintings in various stages of completion—or abandonment—created a maze of wooden stands and canvas squares. Trestan navigated it with practiced ease. Gripping his pistol, he crept further into the home of Josef Danhauser, a young artist fresh from Prague.

A slight squishing sound came from the next room.

Trestan fell still and waited. His eyes adjusted to the lantern's faint light.

Peeking around the corner, he spotted an unmade bed, empty bottles on the nightstand, and rags clogged with paint stains. The squishing continued, like an octopus squeezing life from its prey.

It was Danhauser himself, molding something in a basin. He was young, with a mop of dark hair and thin mustache. Veins stuck out on his forearms.

Several masks were drying on a nearby shelf. Black material, scowling features.

"It's a shame he did not find peace upon his death." Trestan entered, hiding the pistol inside his coat. "Especially when his sadness is molded for all eternity."

Danhauser whirled around, dropping the mask he was working on. It struck the floor with a wet slap, and Beethoven's countenance was scattered over wooden planks. The artist's fine-boned features paled upon sighting Trestan.

"I am working as fast as I can," Danhauser said with defiance. As if he had made the same declaration before. Perhaps even that day.

"But not for me." Trestan offered a smile meant to set people at ease. With it, he had lured men to their deaths, women to their shame, and nations to their ruin.

Danhauser attempted to stand straighter, and stuck out his chin. "Who are you, sir, that you appear in my apartments at such a late hour?"

"The hour is never late." Trestan removed his hat. "Just like the hour wasn't late for your beloved Beethoven. They still sing his praises outside, even now. If we wait three days, will he rise from the dead? Then the Church could have two Easters a year."

"You blasphemous Frenchman," Danhauser muttered.

Trestan pulled back his jacket, revealing the pistol. "Yet those who employed you to make theses masks were less heretical? Tell me about them."

"His family wished a death mask for posterity," Danhauser said.

"I see at least seven copies." Trestan chuckled. "Was he so beloved by his kin, that they all want that wretched face hanging in their lobbies? I think not. You did this work for commission, and so I offer you a new one: your life, for information."

Danhauser's cheeks flushed, and he stared at the floor. "Sir … you are not the first to threaten me."

"No … but I will be the last." Trestan drew the pistol. He didn't want to pull the trigger. The young man would see reason; it would not come to that.

A knock struck the apartment door.

Danhauser eyed Trestan with a scornful question. Trestan pointed at the door, but tapped the pistol. After a curt nod, Danhauser answered the door. Trestan hid behind a curtain in the hall connecting both rooms. With a clear shot at Danhauser's back.

The tuning fork shook in his pocket. Indicating that a meta-phonics user was near.

The pistol shook in his hand as Trestan hid in the cellar beneath the lady's home. In past years she'd supplied him with intelligence regarding who came and went through Paris, but now, the Allies occupied the city. British and German soldiers marched down the streets with the causal arrogance of conquerors. He'd seen his own countrymen swagger into other cities the same way.

Voices in the level above. Her voice, and harsh, German ones. The Frenchman in him detested invaders to his nation, but the coward in him wanted to flee. To live the next day, to sacrifice whoever he must to survive. That was the morality of the spy.

Trestan tried to focus, but his thoughts kept flipping from the past to the present.

She denied Trestan's presence when they asked. The sounds of their palms, and then their fists, connecting with her soft body, made Trestan cringe in a corner. Her screams were soon muffled, but the callous, eager grunts of her violators continued.

Damn that Fouché, why didn't he give more warning about these episodes?

Trestan fantasized about running up there. He could surprise them, save the woman. Many other scenarios played out in his head, but Trestan remained in the cellar, like a bottle of bad wine no one wanted. When it was over, he wiped his cheeks.

So much for the Revolution.

Trestan blinked. He held the tuning fork in a white-knuckle grip, silencing it at last. Talleyrand had called this a vice? Reliving his most emasculating moments?

But wait. Someone was near. Using metaphonics against him.

This time, Trestan wouldn't hesitate. He would pull the trigger.

Danhauser opened the door after the third knock. He stood aside so that Trestan got a clear view of the visitor. The young cur probably hoped to confuse Trestan's aim. But rather than a shadowy figure, something else entirely called upon Danhauser.

A young woman entered, attired in a mourner's dress, complete with veil. She drew the veil aside, revealing high cheekbones, plump lips. Her brown eyes judged Danhauser and the room with a glance. Lustrous brown hair brushed her shoulders.

"Good evening, Herr Danhauser," she said in confident, refined German.

He bowed his head slightly. "Good evening. How may I help you, frau…?"

"Ulrika." She offered a polite smile. "I am a friend of Herr Beethoven's family, and I would see the progress you have made on his death mask."

Color again stained Danhauser's cheeks, and he hesitated. "It is nearly complete. The initial casting was quite successful. If you'll pardon my saying so."

Ulrika entered the studio, though Danhauser hadn't invited her in. She didn't move like other women. There was purpose in her stride. "No pardon is necessary. We all celebrate his life in different ways. Please, may I view your progress? I promised the family I would have word on its construction before the funeral procession."

Danhauser swallowed and rubbed his hands together. "I…very well, miss. Please, follow me." He shot Trestan a cold look as he passed the curtain. When Ulrika came by, he caught her perfume scent, and watched how she studied everything around her. Ordinary people never did that. Only those looking for something.

He now had two targets, but only one shot. The gods were cruel.

As Danhauser showed her the masks. Ulrika looked everywhere else, until her eyes fell upon the curtain shielding Trestan from view. Her gaze lingered too long. Yet, she smiled wider, and laughed deeper, at some silly jest Danhauser made.

Flirting turned to socializing when she asked for a drink, and Danhauser provided. They shared a glass of local blaufränkisch— Trestan could smell the oak and black fruit bouquet—then sat on the couch and discussed Beethoven.

"Please tell his relatives that the mask…the mask will be ready tomorrow." Danhauser's charm faltered as he glanced at the curtain. The stink of anxious sweat was overpowering. But Ulrika drained her glass, kept smiling. He rose to get her another.

Ulrika also rose. "Yes, pour us one more, then I shall have to depart." She studied the curtain again. No smiles now. She was a brave one.

While Danhauser filled their glasses, Ulrika lightly caressed the completed death masks. Her eyes, like amber orbs in the lantern light, shone with great sadness. Trestan couldn't help but be touched by the emotion in her gaze. It was real, for Danhauser wasn't watching, and he doubted she did it for Trestan's benefit.

Regardless, he kept the pistol ready.

When Danhauser returned, Ulrika picked one glass, then took the other.

"Pardon me, I'd forgotten my glass. Perhaps I've had too much already."

"Nonsense!" Danhauser grinned. "Please, one more while we remember this city's greatest genius."

"Yes…" Ulrika took rather unlady-like gulps, and Danhauser blushed hotter. "It was like God's Song, his compositions."

"Indeed…" Danhauser wobbled, and they both laughed. Within a minute, his words slurred. He stumbled into his canvases.

Ulrika watched him with detached concern. "A nice vintage, Herr Danhauser." With her eyes on the curtain, she hummed several low notes while reaching for the masks. Notes from Beethoven's Third Symphony.

A round metal device pulsed in her hand.

Trestan thrust aside the curtain as Ulrika split into multiple versions of herself. His tuning fork vibrated, the ripples from it slowing her movements. She whistled more notes, and a high-pitched whine hurt his ears.

"Stop!" Trestan aimed at one phantom after another.

One Ulrika rushed from the apartment with several masks. Another put a mask on and danced around Trestan. A third finished her wine and laughed, while the fourth Ulrika threw a canvas at Trestan. It all happened in the blink of an eye. If not for his tuning fork, he doubted he would have seen it all.

Trestan grabbed one Ulrika, while threatening another with the pistol. Both faded into nothingness. Ulrika Three leapt out the window. Another ran down the stairs. A fifth Ulrika waved a small device, her smile triumphant. Then, she too disappeared.

Aiming the gun at nothing, Trestan gaped all around. A door shut on the street below, and he ran to the window. Down on the curb, a carriage rolled down the avenue.

By the time he reached the street, the carriage was gone. Not simply obfuscated by night or traffic, but gone. His tuner shook from the ripples of her unusual departure.

Afterward, he sniffed Danhauser's glass, then tasted the artist's wine. Opiates.

She was good, this Ulrika.

Inside Château de Valençay, Fouché slammed his fist onto a desk strewn with maps and astronomical charts. "You let her escape? A mere bitch with a quad oscillator. You were armed. You were prepared. Explain yourself!"

Trestan thrust aside his coat and hat. "I had nothing to combat her techniques, which you damn well know. A pistol is but a child's toy against such adversaries."

"Only in the hands of a child," Fouché said.

Fists balled, Trestan stormed forward. Fouché smiled evilly.

"Stop it, you boorish fools." Talleyrand rose from his sedan chair. "We are all children, fighting over the Chorale's playthings. Trestan, you did not fail entirely. Tell me everything that was said. Every detail you can recall."

Trestan obliged. After years of honing his memory, he could repeat conversations verbatim. Even Napoleon had been impressed with his ability. It had helped the French win the battle at Jena-Auerstedt, and at Wagram. He described Danhauser's studio, the masks, and Ulrika. Talleyrand and Fouché showed much interest in her, but when he mentioned 'God's Song', Talleyrand held up a hand.

"God's Song? Damn the Fates." Talleyrand sat back down and rubbed his chin.

"Damn them all, indeed." Fouché raised an eyebrow. "They are the *Gott Lied*. An arm of the German intelligence dating back to Blucher. They sundered the Chorale, stealing many of its secrets. They even stole Haydn's head, thinking it contained a fragment of the Tenth, rolled up inside the composer's skull."

"That is hearsay," Talleyrand said. "Yet the rest is true. Trestan, tell us more of the effect she activated. The quad oscillator."

Trestan described it again, and both men shared a worried glance.

"Why are those masks so important?" Trestan asked.

"Metaphonics requires its users to achieve peak mental focus, else they could become trapped in time, or enter another era rather than their planned destination." Talleyrand studied the astronomical maps for a moment. "Beethoven was a master. The strength of his will might be present in each mask, granting the user greater focus."

Trestan recalled his own meditative shortcomings. They mustn't know.

"It is time we made another incursion into that desert," Talleyrand said.

Fouché became red-faced. "The new army isn't ready yet."

Talleyrand smoothed his jacket. "Neither is the Russian one, nor *Gott Lied*'s, and look at what they have accomplished. We have no other choice. Time is not an ally of those who use metaphonics; it is a medium. Let us make full use of it."

"But, we cannot—" Fouché started, but Talleyrand waved him off.

"We went back and fetched you from death, didn't we? Summon the rest of *Armée de L'ombre*. We must work in concert." Talleyrand motioned for Trestan to follow. "You will be journeying to a world that the Chorale reached with their powers."

"A…world?" Trestan's skin chilled. "I just watched that pretty *putain* divide herself into five individuals, then vanish in a carriage. I demand to know—"

"You will be disoriented." Talleyrand gripped his shoulder. "You will have doubts. But stay the course, my good man. There are other worlds the Tenth may be hidden on. Other planets Galileo never saw through his trite tube. They must be traversed, before you can reach our enemies…and learn what they have found."

Movement II

4.

Adagio Misterioso in A major, Opus 31
Serapis

Château de Valençay's library was a modern bibliotheca rivaling that of Alexandria. Trestan wondered who among *Armée de L'ombre* had ventured so far back to reclaim some of those lost tomes. He'd expanded his own reading in the years since Napoleon's fall: the works of the ancient Greeks numbered among his favorites. They had imagined a world of perfect marble, aestheticized in the forms of their gods. But like humans, those gods were filled with faults, horrors, and failures. The subtext being that nothing was above corruption and pettiness, not even the divine.

Trestan wanted to raise humanity above such corruption. It was the only way he could atone for his own atrocities. Instead of fire, Prometheus would offer possibility.

Talleyrand, Fouché, and others of *Armée de L'ombre* gathered in the library. He recognized veteran soldiers, former revolutionaries, members of the current Bourbon regime—all dissatisfied with the world they'd been given. They thought he was as zealous as they were. They thought he was a son of the Revolution.

He had betrayed them all. He would set it right.

For so long, Trestan had loved only the Revolution. Now he felt he attended the wake of its funeral, or some forbidden ritual to give it life again. The looks on his comrades' faces revealed that they did not care what it cost. They had never paid the price. Unlike those Spanish civilians years ago, or the hosts killed at Leipzig.

Talleyrand gestured behind a bookcase. "If you are ready?"

"Yes…yes sir." Trestan fidgeted with the uniform they'd provided. Elaborate frogging on his jacket, epaulets on his shoulders, and polished boots made him a dashing Hussar from Imperial days. Its propaganda value wasn't lost on him.

Trestan walked behind the shelves and blinked.

There stood twin columns at least twelve feet high, as wide around as an oak. They appeared Doric in style. Like the many treasures Napoleon sent back home when he invaded Egypt, these too must have been the spoils of the dead emperor. He imagined that pompous face gazing up at it, hating that which was closer to the heavens than he.

"The Chorale, with Beethoven's symphonies, were able to journey to other worlds." Talleyrand accepted a goblet of wine from a servant. The rest of the guests, save for Fouché, also held one, ready to toast him. The beverages fizzled. Champagne.

Fouché approached with an object wrapped in purple velvet. "These worlds can only be reached by using metaphonics. There are rumors of ships that travel the aether separating worlds, but this delicate device is all we have access to. Guard it with your life, Trestan Desaix. It will affect you more than the tuning fork. Keep your wits about you, and do not let your thoughts drift. Focus on where you wish to be."

The old spy unwrapped the velvet, and inside it lay a slim, silver chime. It was engraved with musical notes wrapped around Jupiter and Saturn. Trestan took it and faced the gathering.

They raised their goblets and spoke as one. "Liberty, equality, fraternity!"

"Quintilius Varus, give me back my legions," Trestan whispered.

Trestan saluted them.

The chime rung; a low, docile note, like that of a distant church bell. The sound reverberated within Trestan's body, and he had to force himself not to wobble in place. He stepped between the columns. Talleyrand, the library, and the others faded in and out of reality. Recalling his training, he focused his thoughts on the columns.

Fouché pointed a device with a blinking red light at Trestan. Sections slid apart on the twin columns, revealing intricate machinery and a glowing core of power. Trestan's tuning fork pulsated along with the chime. The note multiplied in strength.

Heart bursting with fear, he sought her in the crowd. But she was gone.

The chime's noise rose in volume, and Trestan fell to his knees, covered his ears. His scream was drowned out by the enormity of the sound, as if he were a fly trapped in the bowels of a great cathedral organ.

Bright, hot light forced Trestan's eyes open. He knelt in a wilderness of sand, between the same two columns from the library. He stared across dunes, distant canyons. A sapphire sky pocked with desiccated clouds.

Wind blew, hot and gritty. Trestan rose, then realized he was still covering his ears. He stretched, feeling he'd slept several hours since he'd stood in Talleyrand's home. He opened his right hand and stared at the silver chime. The engraved musical notes were in different arrangements. The planets were no longer Jupiter and Saturn.

Realization made him shiver. He was alone on another world.

He scaled dune after dune, never spotting a hint of civilization. The sun was merciless, and he unbuttoned his shirt, removed his waistcoat, and used it to fashion a turban. His skin burned. Sand corroded his boots. He licked his lips, wondering why Talleyrand had provided him no supplies.

The tuning fork vibrated in his pocket, and he took it out. A slight ripple spread out from the tines, which he elected to follow. After climbing two more dunes, the fork led him to a round, terraced object that had been dug out of the ground.

It was an amphitheater.

He'd viewed similar structures on missions to Greece, Italy, even the North African coast, but these stones looked far older. He descended the dune, sand sliding all about, and he slipped. Trestan rolled right into the amphitheater. Something twanged when he struck it. He stood, dusted himself off. He'd bumped into a broken cello.

Chipped seats and rusted metal stands surrounded him. Broken musical instruments lay everywhere: violins, flutes, trumpets, busted drums. Each time the wind blew, the force tugged strings, filled mouthpieces, buffeted lambskins. It created a disturbing cacophony. He felt its vibrations, and on impulse, raised the bloody fork.

He took deep breaths. Ignored his sunburn. Concentrated.

The sounds leveled out, and soon, the atonal racket became a swooning harmony. Brittle and arrhythmic, but more pleasing to the ear. He didn't make it so—the tuning fork revealed what was already there.

For hours he rummaged over the site, even peeking inside the instruments. He found a few scraps of manuscript, but none of it was a fragment of the Tenth. Using the bloody fork, he discovered that resonations were stronger on this world. Perhaps that's how Beethoven found it.

While he stood and stretched his back, the gleam of metal caught his eye.

Topping the next dune, Trestan halted and touched his pistol. Down below, dozens of skeletal bodies lay half-buried in the sand. Many wore cuirassier breastplates. Closer inspection revealed that many shared the same metallic countenance he'd faced in Vienna, the night Beethoven's apartment was burned. The rest were human skeletons.

Shivering, he raced back up the dune and lay prone. With cautious eyes he scanned the horizon, the amphitheater, the distant columns. He cocked the pistol.

"It must have been quite a battle," a voice said in German-accented French.

Trestan whirled and aimed.

Ulrika stood atop the next dune, wearing a black, tight-fitting jumpsuit. Her unbound hair blew in the wind. A smirk parted her lips. She aimed a strange gun at him.

"Quite." Trestan gawked at her scandalous attire.

"So they sent you here, thinking to steal it from under my nose?" She sidled down the dune. "What have you found?"

"Nothing." Trestan kept the gun aimed on her. "What is this place?"

Ulrika smiled. "They did not even tell you. That is typical of the men you serve."

"Where?" He stood, slowly. Eyes on her gun.

"They call it Serapis." Ulrika lowered her gun. "We can help each other."

"I doubt that." Trestan tried to appear in control, but he was covered in sweat, while she seemed comfortable. He finally holstered the gun in his belt.

"You Frenchman always doubt everything," Ulrika said. "Voltaire, Descartes, Diderot. You disbelieve your own reality, then try to steal someone else's."

"Speaking of thieves … who did you give the masks to?" Trestan asked.

She paced around him, never taking her eyes off him. "Does it matter? I am here seeking Beethoven's Tenth, like you, Trestan Desaix."

"Who do you serve? The Russians?"

Ulrika stopped pacing. "Here, on Serapis, we are bound to no one. Let them fight their little wars. Let us discover what comes next."

Trestan wiped his brow. "How did the Chorale find such a place? Is this truly another world?"

"Look." Ulrika pointed.

There were three moons in the sky. One light blue, one gray, and the other a deep red. Different sizes, different phases.

"Beethoven unlocked so many secrets of the universe with his music," Ulrika said. "How many have your superiors shown you?"

Trestan scowled. "How much will yours let you have, once this is all over?"

"Over?" Ulrika walked between the lifeless soldiers. "It never ends. See here their automatons, their wars carried over to these new worlds. Is that what the Revolution wants, Trestan? Is that what you want?"

"Do you serve *Gott Lied*?"

"Do you serve that silly Army of the Shadows?"

"Shadow Army," he corrected her.

"Do you want what Beethoven created before he died?" Ulrika raised her brows.

"First … tell me what happened here. And why." He kicked aside a metal carcass.

"The Chorale kept its secrets to itself," she said. "That's why their music was accessible only to the rich, the aristocracy. Men. You should know all about that."

"Don't judge me," he said. "Go on."

"Beethoven changed that. He sought to spread his music, and his secrets, to everyone. Not all agreed." Ulrika meandered through the metallic cadavers. "When the Chorale split, they fought on our world, and others, like this one. Fought for Beethoven's legacy, and the whereabouts of his most powerful work. Metaphonics provided the knowledge to build these false soldiers. No flesh, no mind, no soul—they are as dispensable as they are deadly."

"How many factions are there?" Trestan kept pace with her. He'd not lose her again. She was his only lead.

"At least three. Perhaps four, but since time is so malleable now, one faction might have been destroyed while we walked here and discussed the obvious." Ulrika stopped and regarded him. "This quest, like music, is not meant for solitary endeavor."

"Music is useless unless it is heard," Trestan said.

"Exactly." She smiled. "Do you hear that?"

Trestan went still. "What?"

She produced a tuning fork from her jumpsuit. It vibrated visibly, the tines blurring into one another as she held it up to the horizon.

After a moment, he heard it too; it resembled the broken harmony he'd heard at the amphitheater, but stronger. He held up his own fork. It vibrated the same way.

"Beethoven learned how to measure the vibration of sound, of light," Ulrika said. "The music of the spheres, Haydn called it. These devices detect it. Together, we might learn its location." She stepped closer to him, and their forks almost touched.

"Careful, your tuner—"

Trestan gasped.

Smoke cleared, revealing more carcasses. Imperial Guardsmen, Russian infantry, Prussian jägers. Shattered muskets, smoldering cannons. Craters filled with limbs. Trestan dismounted and walked through the corpses, squishing through viscera. Flies buzzed in miniature black storms on the dead, and the cries of vultures was a foul opera.

"Trestan?"

Ulrika's voice was drowned out as the wounded screamed for water. One Russian fended off a vulture from the bodies of his comrades, even as he bled his life out via a severed leg. Trestan sloshed through red pools trapped between bodies, like a seashore at low tide. Hands clawed up after him, begging for water, for mercy. Begging for death.

Ignoring them, Trestan led his mount through the remains of Probstheida. Before the battle, it had been a village. Now it was a graveyard, the gutted buildings clogged with the dead. The setting sun tinted all banners and uniforms the ruby shade of Ares.

"Stay with me!" She shook him.

Serving as a scout, Trestan noted the French's precarious position on the battlefield. The Grande Armée was exhausted, outnumbered, and outgunned. Napoleon would have to retreat from Leipzig, most likely on the morrow. After completing his reconnaissance for Marshal MacDonald, Trestan reached for his horse's bridle.

A pistol fired. The horse whinnied and collapsed. Trestan stumbled and fell, gloves sliding off bloodied forms. A Russian officer staggered over, saber raised.

"You devil," Trestan said in broken Russian. "Why my horse?"

"I aimed for you." The Russian loomed over him. "You won't escape this time."

Ulrika slapped him. "You must focus on the tuner's correct vibration, on this reality! Else you will be trapped between them, and no one can reach you."

Trestan was once again on Serapis. Looking up at Ulrika.

Though he remembered that terrible evening at Leipzig, there had never been a Russian officer stalking him. He'd remounted, rode to MacDonald, made his report. Perhaps metaphonics toyed with his memories, or the desert sun addled him.

"Whom have you promised my head…Salome?" Trestan grinned. It came more natural to him than any other expression, and that robbed it of his genuine thankfulness.

Ulrika studied him, her unreadable eyes full of weight. Then she smiled back, an easy, crooked smile that was the most charming thing he'd ever seen.

"Why, the future, my Baptist." Ulrika helped him stand straight. "Though I am not dancing in this heat."

"You seem unaffected by it." Trestan eyed her jumpsuit. "Is that of this world?"

"It is something the Chorale fashioned that lets humans survive longer. That is why the sun doesn't burn me."

They continued over the dunes, past two more old battlefields of metal soldiers, and between a shattered arch that might have seen the triumphs of kings.

"Humans did not build all of this," Trestan said.

"Perhaps." Ulrika pointed over the horizon. "There. Another amphitheater."

They hurried on, but Trestan's body had perspired much of its water, and he was sluggish and fatigued. Ulrika kept watching him until she finally handed him a small square device. It blinked green.

"What is this?"

"It will give you strength." Without further explanation, she rummaged among the amphitheater's musical instruments and scattered costumes. After a few minutes, Trestan regained energy, and was able to help. He had more questions, but Ulrika was too engrossed in their hunt. They were rivals, seeking a treasure these armies had overlooked.

He didn't trust her. Yet her presence made Serapis bearable. He kept searching.

Their search revealed nothing. Frustrated, Ulrika pulled out her tuner and sang a few perfect, dulcet notes. Trestan watched in simple adoration; he'd heard few people with such vocal control, especially in an arid locale.

"You are a performer?" he asked.

"We are all performers." She watched the tuner's vibration. It reacted to her voice, but still lacked something. Another harmony…

Trestan used his tuner, recalling the vibration he'd made in the other amphitheater. The two devices, working in concert, pulsated. A powerful aural ripple cascaded over the desert landscape. Sand stirred from the dunes.

Cobblestones in the center of the amphitheater rose and spread apart. Keyed to the frequency emitted by the devices, they confirmed what Trestan had suspected all along—the Tenth would not be found by merely searching libraries, diaries, and folios.

They shared a look, then smiled.

She hurried forward and reached into the opening. A metal cylinder lay inside. Trestan trailed after, hand near his pistol. The game was almost up.

Ulrika spoke without turning. "I saved you from shifting through time. You might still be back there, imagining yourself in the past, or the future."

"And you have my thanks." Trestan aimed the pistol. "But not my prize."

"Do not be so premature." She turned, holding his silver chime. They'd been in close enough proximity for her to steal it a dozen times. It pulsed at her touch.

He cocked the hammer, more annoyed than angry. "You'll not abandon me here."

Ulrika opened the cylinder. Inside was a rolled-up manuscript—written in Beethoven's hand. Though incomplete, he knew, from his studies—and Fouché's briefings—that it was an unknown composition.

"A fragment of the Tenth … perhaps the second movement." Ulrika replaced it into the cylinder. "I'm sure your superiors will send someone to collect you."

There would only be once chance to stop her.

She rose, her crooked grin eliciting one from him—but for a very different reason.

Trestan flicked his tuner, then muted one of the tines with his thumb. The vibration was reversed, and the cobblestone pit closed back up—around Ulrika.

Struggling against the stones, she drew her strange gun. He kicked it from her grasp, then snatched after the chime. Ulrika pulled him into the pit with her as it sealed over. Tangled together, they were pressed down by the stones. Rumbling noises drowned out their cries, then they were in the dark, trapped in the round, compact space.

"You fool!" she cried. "Now we'll both die on this miserable world!"

The chime glowed faintly. Trestan reached for it, but her elbow bumped him.

His pistol discharged. The sound deafened them. Smoke from the powder made them cough. She pressed against him, and he nudged back. Finally, his hearing returned.

"Huh?" She mashed her palm into his chest, gaining no traction.

"I said, were you shot?"

"Now you care?" She grunted in frustration. "Hand me the chime!"

"I told you … you'll not abandon me here."

Ulrika muttered a curse, then whistled low. The square device she'd given him sent a jolt into his body. He gasped and quivered, but still held the chime.

"You lied about that thing?" Trestan squirmed to no avail. His nerves were numb.

"The chime, or we'll both perish here." The confidence in her tone was gone.

"Why? And why should I trust you?"

"Because you want to see for yourself." He glimpsed her face in the chime's faint light. Nostrils flaring, jaw tight. Defiant to the last.

He snorted. "And what is that?"

"The future."

The air grew thinner, and he finally nodded. They both gripped the chime. Ulrika recited quick, sharp notes, and device shook. In a ripple of energy, they departed Serapis.

5.

Allegro Grandioso in G major, Opus 31
1854
Paris

Trestan doubled over and retched. The chime pulsed so hard, his hand numbed.

"Gather your wits before you attract attention." Ulrika steered him out of a carriage's path as it rushed down an avenue. Passersby gave him curious stares.

Straightening, Trestan recognized the Arc de Triomphe in the distance. Only, in his time, it had remained incomplete. Now it stood tall and glorious over Parisian streets.

His beloved city looked familiar, and he smelled the aromas of fresh loaves in a nearby bakery, something that'd always welcomed him home. But there were newer, taller buildings, and more traffic on the Champs-Élysées. People wore different clothes. Dark smoke drifted with the breeze, carrying the stink of scorched metal and coal.

"I said, are you well?" Ulrika wore a low-necked dress with a white chemisette, and a lace bonnet bedecked with violet primula flowers. Her chestnut hair was plaited across her head, round two buns. Smirking, she nodded to his own person.

He himself was dressed in a fine navy blue suit, complete with top hat, turnover collars, and low-heeled shoes. The ensemble's domesticity irritated him.

"How?" he asked.

"That resonator you have—the chime—focuses on the ripples of the target era, allowing us to blend in," Ulrika said. "Metaphonics, like music, appreciates harmony."

"But how distant is this era?" He rubbed his shaven jaw, realizing every other man sported elaborate mustaches, beards, and sideburns.

"The year of our lord, eighteen fifty-four." She took his arm. "Come."

Though his eyes drank in the sights, Trestan's mind reeled. 1854…were Talleyrand, Fouché, and the rest still alive? How long would this conflict last?

"I don't trust you." He slid the chime into his pocket.

"When has a man ever trusted a woman? You pretend you are different, with your ideals, but you are the same as other men, Trestan Desaix."

Trestan's cheeks burned. "I pretend nothing. Were I the same, I'd have shot you in the back on Serapis, rather than negotiate."

Ulrika dug her nails into his hand. "You call that negotiating?"

"When we are both still alive afterwards…yes." He smiled.

"You are an arrogant fool." She smiled at other Parisians, still clasping his arm.

"Then this must be torturous for you," he said. "Needing a fool like me."

She shot him a look, then disengaged herself when they neared the next building. It was a run-down apartment, with trash on the steps.

"Who lives here?" Trestan gazed up at windows covered in dark drapes.

"An old friend." Ulrika's voice was wistful. "He will help you understand what your countrymen have refused to show."

It was a ploy among those whose currency was secrecy: convince a rival that their comrades kept secrets from them. Trestan wasn't fooled. They were all using each other.

Once inside, he found the interior cloying. Every wall was covered with paintings, each table housed a sculpture or clock. Busts of

Greek deities, bronzes of mythological monsters, and paintings of a doe-like woman with brown hair gave the impression of a museum rather than a residence. Everything stank of must, and a layer of dust coated all.

For Trestan, it evoked a nostalgic pining for what was, but what would never be.

The strains of piano echoed through the dwelling, often starting with a complex harmony, then ending in atonal discordance, as if the player got frustrated and mashed the keys. He glanced at Ulrika, but her eyes were for everything but him: examining any life-size statues, and avoiding curtains or closets. Friend or not, she feared something.

The playing faltered as they entered a parlor, its windows thrust open to the racket of Parisian thoroughfares. The mishmash of horses, carriages, and voices created a counterpoint to the broken performance. A denial of entropy in the adlib corpus, more than the clothing or dirty air, made Trestan feel a man out of his time.

The recitalist paused and slowly turned. He had full, curly grey hair, swept to the side as if he'd just ridden a flying carpet. Once flawless, his suit displayed signs of moth damage. His aged face bore far less years than his heavy-lidded eyes. Eyes that had seen the sundering of Ur, eyes that had beheld Constantinople's triple cordoned walls. Yet upon seeing Ulrika, the old man leapt from the piano and embraced her like a father.

"Henriette, my dear, you haven't aged a day! You presence is like the dawning of spring in these halls. As you no doubt heard, my piano playing is still abysmal."

So she used aliases. Considering the old man's reaction, he'd known Ulrika by that moniker for a very long time. Longer than the cover of an alias would require.

"Hello, my friend." Ulrika drew back and indicated Trestan. "This is Trestan Desaix, a fellow musical enthusiast. Trestan, this is Hector Berlioz, the head librarian at the Paris Conservatoire. Sometimes he composes." They shared a smile at that comment.

Trestan noticed many of the room's pictures were of the same woman. Her hair was the same shade as Ulrika's. A shiver crawled up his back.

Berlioz caught Trestan looking at the paintings, and sighed. "Yes, my late wife, Harriet. I lost her this year. It has been hard, composing of late."

"My condolences, sir," Trestan said.

Berlioz nodded, then smiled at Ulrika. "So, tell me: are you here on tour? I hear that Wagner is seeking a soprano for another one of his mystical operas."

"Tour?" Trestan raised an eyebrow at her.

"Why, of course." Berlioz grinned. "She was one of the sopranos that sung at the first performance of Beethoven's Ninth Symphony. By my life, I still cannot believe how young you look. So tell me, what can I do for you?"

Ulrika's smile waned. "Berlioz…Trestan is a practitioner of metaphonics."

"I have no idea what you're talking about…my dear." Berlioz stiffened.

"He knows about the Tenth," Ulrika said.

Berlioz's demeanor resumed the forlorn countenance he'd worn upon their arrival. "I asked you to maintain the pretense we had agreed upon, Henriette."

Ulrika removed her bonnet and tossed it onto the piano. Dust filled the air. "You see that? That is time passing you by. You cannot ignore what you know is true."

Trestan felt a slight pulse from his tuner, but remained still.

"Tragedy is all I know these days." Berlioz slammed the cover over the piano keys. "You would do well to cease this quest. You have so much ahead of you—"

"This is the year I was supposed to die," Ulrika said.

Trestan and Berlioz flinched, then glanced at each other.

"But…how are you here?" Berlioz shook his head. "Each individual must return to their time stream, it cannot be changed—"

"*Gott Lied* helped me contain that vibration in the cosmic stream." She flushed.

Berlioz groaned and leaned on the piano. "You know what their goals are. What did you give them in return?"

"It doesn't matter." Ulrika pulled out her oscillator. "Don't you see? Beethoven's enemies haven't stopped. They are utilizing the scraps they've collected, the ones they stole years ago when Schubert was murdered."

"Wait," Trestan said. "Are you saying you are immortal? What matters death, if you can travel through time?"

"Metaphonics is a science, not sorcery." Berlioz glared at him. "So you are a practitioner, you know of the Tenth, yet you are ignorant of your own vibrations in space-time? Who are you, really, sir?"

"His is of *Armée de L'ombre*." Ulrika shut the window. "We must hurry."

Trestan regarded her with angry bewilderment. "Why tell him?"

Berlioz yanked a conductor's wand from his jacket. "You trust this man, Ulrika? *Armée de L'ombre* hasn't given up, either. Who do you think has sabotaged my reputation, here in my own homeland?"

A cold ball formed in Trestan's stomach. "Sir, I encountered Ulrika on the world of Serapis. We recovered a fragment of the Tenth there."

"Indeed?" Hope grew in Berlioz's eyes, then his expression darkened. He aimed the wand at Trestan. "Show it to me."

"Stop." Ulrika placed herself between the wand and Trestan.

Berlioz scowled, then finally sighed and lowered the wand.

"There is still a chance to set things right." Ulrika gently massaged Berlioz's shoulder. "Please ... now is not the time to give up."

"The revolution Beethoven sought died years ago," Berlioz said.

"No," Trestan said. "The Revolution is within us. That's what holds my loyalty. Not *Armée de L'ombre* and their rotting politicos." Lie or not, the words felt right.

"Please." Ulrika squeezed Berlioz's shoulder.

Years weighed down Berlioz as he sat at the piano. "I sacrificed so much in my quest to assemble it. I included pieces of the fragments

I found in my own compositions. It is not enough. We need another genius to come along, to show us the way."

"We cannot wait," Trestan said. "We have a fragment from Serapis. What other worlds did the Chorale find?"

"Many," Berlioz said. "But wars have already been fought on them."

"This one can still be saved." Trestan felt more emboldened by the minute. Here he was, in a future where his superiors still hadn't won, where France thrived. It proved Talleyrand was wrong: *Armée de L'ombre* didn't want the Tenth to guarantee French prosperity and survival; they wanted it to build another Empire. The very thing that had stolen, then slain, the Revolution. Trestan would have no part of it.

Berlioz looked at them both. "I know of a place. Reaching it will take some preparation. Enemies still lurk out there in the time streams, waiting for the right vibration to summon them to us uninvited. I will need to focus."

"How long?" Trestan peered out the window.

"For tonight." Berlioz accepted Ulrika's aid in helping him up. "Metaphonics isn't activated with a button, such as *Gott Lied* believes, or a craft to be mastered, like *Armée de L'ombre* thinks. Metaphonics is like a river. You must learn to navigate it."

"Do you have any allies in this city?" Trestan asked. "Any defenses here?"

Berlioz shrugged. "My enemies have already defeated me where it counts. They will not come after us here. It is on other worlds where they willingly sacrifice everything for small gain. Please, make yourselves at home. Ulrika trusts you, and so I must. I will be in my bedroom. Please, do no disturb me. We depart in the morning."

Trestan waited until the old composer left the room, then neared Ulrika and whispered. "My tuner vibrated. Despite what he says, there are enemies out there."

"Of course there is." She checked her oscillator. "We must keep watch, while he prepares. Can you manage without sleep? Or is the rumor of the lazy Frenchman true?"

"No more than that of the industrious, hard-assed German."

They traded stares. Finally, she smirked. "Touché."

Berlioz's larder featured a bottle of Pinot Noir, bread loaves, Gouda cheese, and apricots, on which they feasted. While Ulrika explained how metaphonics increased caloric intake and metabolism, Trestan was stumped by her concise knowledge. He'd met women from all stations of society, aristocrats to harlots, and none were like her.

"What does your husband think of your immoral escapades?" Trestan asked.

Ulrika pelted him with a bread heel. "Can't I be something else than a wife?"

He smiled at her ire. "My mother thought the same. She braved the Bastille, losing an eye for her trouble. But she was proud. Thus I was reared by revolutionaries."

"How would she feel, knowing you nearly shot a woman in the back?"

"She…loathed the type of man I've become." Trestan stared at his unfinished wine. "We brought down kings, swore to ensure equality, and yet served an emperor who changed mistresses like he changed clothes."

"That is what your masters wish to restore." She raised an eyebrow. "And you?"

"I am not them." Trestan downed the wine and paced the room.

In the bedroom, Berlioz played a guitar, displaying much greater ability for it than the piano. The piece evoked a flight of fancy, of fairies dancing in emerald glades.

Ulrika removed her chemisette, loosened her bodice. "I loathe this clothing."

"Not to mention decency." Trestan removed his own jacket and waistcoat.

"I've never heard a Frenchman complain about the risqué or the macabre." Ulrika offered her hand. The music continued. Infectious, focused. Never-ending.

Her confidence mocked him, dared him. Just like a true revolutionary.

"That is because we don't complain." Trestan accepted her hand and led her into a dance. She took to the movement as naturally as a bird to flight. They capered round the parlor, eyes locked as the game between them continued. Her dancing was perfection, twisting and pirouetting away from him. Trestan summoned old dancing skills that served him well in the courts of Europe. Many a mission was completed by winning over a fine damsel on the dance floor, or introducing some general to a lady in exchange for strategic hints. Dancing was as natural as sex, primal provocation between two animals. Trestan reveled in it, and from her hungry eyes, so did Ulrika.

"If not matrimonial servitude, what does a famed soprano seek in the Tenth?"

She laughed at his question. "Everything our world lacks."

"This metaphonics lets us travel through time, creates double of ourselves, grants a peek at future technology…what will the Tenth do, if fully assembled and performed?"

"No one truly knows." Ulrika smirked. "That is why everyone wants it."

Trestan frowned. "So you risk all that you are on such a fragile gamble? What if the Tenth Symphony is worthless, or a hoax?"

"Even so, I would see the Tenth safe from those who'd exploitit."

As they danced, Berlioz's playing quickened in tempo, and the parlor grew warm. Stifling. Ulrika loosened her clothing, Trestan tugged off his necktie. It glided between them, an ephemeral gauntlet thrown down in challenge to see who could outdo the other.

The necktie floated down, winnowing through reality like a banner. A flag of truce; a rag of surrender. Trestan focused on it as the music vibrated his person.

Vibrated his tuner.

Trestan's hand shot to his pocket where the chime was hidden, but he wasn't in the parlor anymore. Instead of Ulrika dancing with him, he clasped the hand of a wobbling, dying soldier.

He didn't recognize the landscape, one of rolling hills and a river. The soldier was Russian, wearing a green and white uniform with a black feathered hat.

All around lay hundreds of dead Russian troops. Arrayed in lines even in death, perishing one rank at a time. On the slope below, hundreds of French lay dead or dying. The collective groans of both nationalities created a language even animals recognized. Vultures and crows circled overhead, having heard the tongue of the dying.

Shattered cannons and caissons lay among the blasted remains of artillery horses. Some of the legs still twitched, the nervous system active despite death. Clouds of smoke roiled over the battlefield, and the awful stink of scorched blood and released bowels made Trestan gag. The soldier looked back at him, then fell dead before he could give word to the question in his eyes.

"You see them, Desaix?"

The brusque voice made him turn. There stood the same Russian lieutenant, holding the saber and smoking pistol. Tall and chesty, with black hair and mustache, he looked every inch a Muscovite prince. His steely eyes regarded Trestan as offal.

"Who are you?" Trestan cried. "I have never seen you before!"

"You see how many of my countrymen perished, because of your dwarf king? You see how many were butchered here at Borodino? I carried Bagration off the field myself, before your comrades swarmed the redoubt. Stand up and die like a man, damn you!"

"How?" was all Trestan could manage, as his necktie rode the breeze between them. It was blood-stained and blackened by gunpowder soot. "Who are you?"

"You see the fruits of your revolution, and that is all you can ask?" The officer laughed. "I am Maryshka Ulyanov."

Trestan glanced everywhere for a weapon. "How did you bring me here?"

"You stumble blindly into what they want you to do, Desaix. But please, continue. Each vibration you disturb leads me closer." Maryshka held up a tuner.

"To what gain?" Trestan snatched a pistol off a dead carabiner, but it was empty.

"Gain?" Maryshka reloaded his gun. "I will not allow this to happen to my countrymen again. I will rise up each time and destroy your Shadow Army."

"I don't serve them anymore…" Trestan tripped over a French officer, half of his face blown away by cannon fire.

"Neither do you serve yourself." Maryshka fired.

Trestan collapsed in Ulrika's arms, clutching his chest.

6.

Andante in F major, Opus 31
Eurytion

The guitar's melody enveloped Trestan, separating him from the reality in Paris to others adjacent in space-time. In one, he lay on the shore of great ocean. He sat in the Theater am Kärntnertor, where Ulrika delivered an ecstatic aria. He hung crucified on a hillock overlooking a village in Palestine, where children threw stones at him until Roman soldiers scared them off. Each era's vibration resembled his, but none were truly him. He recalled Fouché's instruction: the vibration of gravity and light, through time and space, was a delicate affair, and required a trained mind.

"Focus the note," Berlioz said.

Trestan tried to move, but he was trapped between moments. It was the only way he could describe it. Caught outside the realm of time. Yet his mind continued to work, an agonizing state akin to watching ice melt over the course of a millennium. He saw Ulrika standing beside him, he spotted a ring of standing stones, and he glimpsed Berlioz's face, but all else was stars, galaxies, and the tremor of his own stream in the universe.

"Focus!" Berlioz cried.

The stream shook gently, rather than violently, like when Maryshka shot him, or when he kept returning to the carnage at Salamanca. Was so much of his existence centered on death and bloodshed? He was more than a catalyst for destruction. His missions had saved lives, he'd secured victories for his Emperor…

Hands unbuttoned his shirt, felt his pulse. Examined his chest where Maryshka shot him. But there was no hole, no wound.

As a new vibration nudged him from the stream, Trestan tried recalling those who meant something to him. Both parents had died long ago, and his cousin Louis fell at Marengo. No wife, no long-time lovers…just the Revolution.

"Trestan?"

He opened his eyes. He lay on a rock slab, centered in a ring of stones atop a mountain. It reminded him of the Carnac stones in Brittany, back when he was a boy visiting relatives. The sky was light violet, no clouds. A band of bright blue, orange, and red stretched vertically, from horizon to the heavens. It resembled a rainbow, but fuller, more corporeal, and far more distant. Trees and grass crowned the mountain's summit.

Ulrika stood over him.

"Damn him," Trestan breathed.

"Berlioz deserves your gratitude." Ulrika glared. "He stabilized your stream."

"Not him." Trestan coughed. "That Russian. Ulyanov…from Leipzig…"

"Easy. You're not in the past now." Dressed in revealing silks and leather bodice, Ulrika kept manipulating her oscillator. He himself wore a silken vest and a leather skirt of pteruges, like some Roman statue of yore.

Touching his chest, Trestan still felt bruised. "Can one die in these time streams?"

"Yes. That is why you must stay focused." Ulrika sighed and shook the oscillator.

He got off the stone slab, feeling too much a sacrificial victim there.

Berlioz stood nearby, conducting an orchestra—without any musicians. The instruments, carved from exotic woods, stood upright on a pedestal before each empty seat. Nevertheless, with each wave of his conducting wand, Berlioz teased a performance from the ensemble. Invisible hands fretted the strings, moved the bows, gave breath to brass and woodwinds. Soon, Ulrika's voice accompanied the piece, an aria gently soaring to the strange rainbow overhead. He sensed its ripples as his tuner reacted.

"What is this place?" Trestan asked when they finished.

"Eurytion." Berlioz lowered his wand. "The Chorale used it as a staging ground to more distant worlds. With these orchestra pits, metaphonic amplifiers that are many times more powerful than a mere tuner or oscillator, one could move a city through time or space. Eurytion was found when Beethoven premiered his Sixth Symphony."

Trestan laughed despite himself. "So you're telling me that Beethoven arrived on this world, disappearing from the *Theater an der Wien* while the orchestra kept playing?"

Ulrika gave a scolding look. "You should know better. Beethoven could occupy more than one stream, like we are, while our alter egos dwell in past and future ones."

"Is that how Fouché still lives, after the year of his death?" Trestan neared her and lowered his voice. "Is that how you are alive?"

Ulrika hesitated and looked away, but Berlioz regarded her sternly.

"We have shown him this much, and you urged me to bring you both here."

"I changed my stream," Ulrika finally said, staring into space.

"How?" Trestan leaned against a stone and crossed his arms.

"By making the vibration of my existence sustain itself indefinitely. Like *Armée de L'ombre* did to Fouché."

"What are the consequences of that?" Trestan asked.

Berlioz didn't look at Ulrika. "That person will never be grounded in one time stream for long. They are unable to remain static beings. They flit through reality like a firefly in the night. Eventually, they fade from their original era, as if they never existed."

"Spare us the poetry." Ulrika paced around the stones. "I remain human in every other way. I grow bored easily, so this suits me."

Trestan wondered why she'd made such a sacrifice. Living forever, but no one would remember her. Removed from all that had created her, everything and everyone she'd ever encountered, loved, or hated. An exile in space-time.

Studying the sky, Ulrika still radiated defiance, despite her moist gaze.

Eager to break the silence, he pointed at the otherworldly rainbow. "What's that?"

"Those are planetary rings," Ulrika said. "They vibrate most beautifully."

"The very voice of the firmament." Berlioz's smile belonged to a younger man.

Trestan realized they'd seen many more places like this, possessing knowledge he'd never dreamed of. Europe's conflicts were trite by comparison. It was beyond a mere revolution—it was power once ascribed to God. But that concept, like the craft of metaphonics, was created by humanity. The ultimate empowerment.

Ulrika was more than human: she was between moments. Cheating time itself.

He caught her watching him, then she walked behind another stone.

"Is this the only way to reach these worlds?" Trestan gestured at the orchestra.

"No." Ulrika appeared from behind the plinth before him. "I have seen fragile metal ships, hurtling to distant stars."

Trestan grunted. "If we can be any time, any place, why here? Why would Beethoven secure his last symphony in such places?"

"Finally." Ulrika's oscillator pulsed, and her outfit transformed into the black jumpsuit she'd wore on Serapis. "The Chorale set certain defaults to each world it discovered. They thought Eurytion a fairyland. Visitors are dressed accordingly."

"And me?" Trestan pointed at his clothes. Ulrika shrugged and smirked.

Berlioz's wand hummed once. "The preparations are complete. We can be about our business here, but hurry. Others will have felt the tremors in the streams."

Trestan and Ulrika searched around the stone circle, while Berlioz tapped his wand against each plinth, listening for a sound Trestan couldn't hear. Recalling how they'd found the fragment on Serapis, Trestan brought out his tuner, and, together with the chime, discovered a vibration unlike any other.

"Down there." He followed the tuner's signal around the circle, until they ascertained it was but the zenith of a larger structure. The half-buried megalith stretched down the mountainside and onto a flood plain below. It resembled the bones of an ancient city, and between the skeletal frames lay hundreds of metal bodies and human bones.

"Quintilius Varus, give me back my legions," Trestan whispered.

"Other treasure seekers?" He blinked away the memory and indicated the bodies.

Touching stone after stone, she said nothing.

"You think we will share their fate?" Her silence annoyed him, and he blocked her path. "Do you?"

She pushed past him. "Things aren't as black and white as your Revolution claims. You must unlearn what they taught you. What they made you."

"What did they make you?" Trestan grabbed her wrist. "You can't stay in one place? With those you care about, those you love?"

"Let go." Her tone was deadlier than Fouché could manage on his best day.

"They did it against your wishes, didn't they? *Gott Lied.* Didn't they? That's why you collected those masks for them."

"What do you care?" Ulrika pried from his grip. "You've made a career of lying!"

"Because I cannot fathom why you would waste your life like I have!" Trestan loosed a deep breath, then turned to stomp back up the mountain.

Her fingers dug into his shirt, pulling him back. "You don't know me."

"I don't care."

Ulrika kissed him.

She tasted ripe, hot. Thrilling him unlike any woman before. They embraced, leaning on each other's strength, creating a different vibration between them.

He sat in the audience as Ulrika, now Henriette Sontag, sang her part in the Ninth Symphony's fourth movement. So perfect and young as she raised her voice to the sky. A declaration of youth and hope, immortalized in Beethoven's crowning achievement. The deaf composer conducted the orchestra out of time, while another conductor kept the true tempo and pace. But Ulrika was above all of that, her voice soaring into the cosmos along with Beethoven's composition, opening gateways to other worlds, sending humans across the stars. Time became as malleable as water, as smoke, as blood; and through it, he sensed the orgasmic feeling that overcame Ulrika as she realized it, too. She was an angel, wings alight with the fiery magnificence of birth.

Her fingers kneaded through his hair, his lips glided down her neck. Finally they knelt in the grass, grounding their lust in Eurytion's primeval vastness.

The audience stirred. Ulrika kept singing as the Ninth drew to its conclusion, but Trestan stood. Figures in black masks moved forward, brandishing weapons. Daggers, pistols, devices he wasn't familiar with. She was ignorant of them, so caught up in her performance. As blind to her danger as the genius was deaf to his creation.

Ulrika withdrew her lips as the ground shuddered. "What's this?"

Trestan started to rush the stage, but a strong hand restrained him.

"This is but one stream, one note in the vibration of the universe," Maryshka said, attired in the clothes of a rich gentleman. "You cannot change them all."

While the other soprano, Caroline Unger, turned Beethoven around to see his audience's ecstatic applause, the masked figures carried off Ulrika. They already disappeared between time's ripples. Trestan reached for her, but Maryshka held him.

A stone pit, much like the one on Serapis, opened. Ulrika dug a metal cylinder from it. It contained a fragment of the Tenth.

"I had to," she whispered.

Trestan's tuner emitted a vibration like the one he'd felt in Vienna. He jumped up.

Figures in black crept among the ruins. Wearing masks.

"Berlioz!" Trestan shouted as he yanked Ulrika to her feet. "Hurry!"

"The *Gott Lied*," Ulrika said.

"You brought them here, didn't you?" Trestan tugged her along, refusing to believe what his heart told him. Refusing to let her go.

Above them, in the circle of stones, Berlioz shouted something. A warbling noise filled the air. As they finally reached the summit, bullets ricocheted off the megaliths.

Maryshka waited inside the stone circle, aiming a machine-like pistol at them. His smile was gracious, but his eyes were frigid coals. "I warned you, Desaix."

"Henriette, go!" Berlioz cried, the wand pulsing in his grasp.

Before Maryshka fired, Trestan focused on the ripples around the circle. Using the chime, he maneuvered between them. One second he stood near Ulrika. The next, he appeared right beside Maryshka and swatted aside the pistol. The shot went astray.

Ulrika activated her oscillator, then five versions of herself ran about the summit. The *Gott Lied* clambered closer. All the while, Berlioz swung his wand as if conducting a symphony of madness. The orchestra obeyed, playing a darker, more frenetic piece.

Trestan swung at Maryshka, but the Russian pummeled him to the ground. He writhed in the grass, even as Maryshka shot one, then another, version of Ulrika. The remaining doppelgangers continued running, until one with the cylinder disappeared.

Dozens of *Gott Lied* swarmed the summit, then faded from existence as the orchestra's melody reached a crescendo. Berlioz waved the wand once more, then grinned at Trestan. "They have forgotten who I am, I think."

Trestan tried to rise, but the crack of a pistol stopped him.

Berlioz wobbled, frowned, then collapsed. His wand rolled away in the grass. Blood spread over his moth-eaten garments, then he, too, disappeared.

Maryhska stared down at Trestan. "She has two fragments now, Desaix. Do you even know who she will give them to?" He aimed the pistol.

"Another day, cretin."

As Maryshka turned, Fouché fired a small curved gun. It shot a bright yellow beam, and Maryshka was gone. The ground smoldered where he'd been standing.

Trestan got to his knees, head swimming with pain. "Thank the Fates…"

Fouché grabbed Berlioz's wand and aimed the gun at Trestan. "Tell me what Ulrika whispered with those pretty lips of hers."

7.

Scherzo in C minor, Opus 31
December 5th, 1791
Vienna

*T*restan stumbled across the dunes after the figure, who was so far away now that the person was little more than a speck on the horizon. His skin was blistered, his lips had crusted shut. Another hour or two, and he would perish in this hellish wasteland.

"Serapis was the Greek god of resurrection and abundance," a stentorian German voice said. "Only a fool would have christened that place as such."

Trestan collapsed at the base of the next dune and rolled onto his side. Sunlight reflected off the trio of moons, an unholy trinity witnessing his death. Or maybe it was the Furies, Alecto, Megaera, and Tisiphone, with the rays of the sun their fiery whips.

"She was there," Fouché said. "Your little songbird led him straight to the damned thing. I thought you had her under control?"

Sand-filled wind scoured away Trestan's flesh. Never had he begged so much for the cold mercy of night. When it finally came, he couldn't even offer a groan in thanks. The lunar triumvirate shone down on him, their different shades making it seem he lay at the bottom of a kaleidoscope, its colored glass scattering the moonlight.

A tender hand touched his face, then a finger dabbed cool, wondrous moisture across his lips. Trestan moaned and tried to see his benefactor, but his eyes had sealed shut, cemented by grime and sand.

"Do you command the sun, the sea, the stars? Spare me your criticisms, Fouché."

Fouché grunted. "You have languished too long, without challengers. That has come to an abrupt end. She is furthering that end."

Trestan sat up. He was now between the two stone columns. Footprints marked the sand up to the space between the columns, then disappeared.

Something hard pressed into Trestan's side. "One move, and you are dead."

Fouché stood over him in an unkempt home, where messily written manuscript pages littered the floor. Trestan lay on a couch covered in wine and food stains. The smell of sickness and alcohol stung his nose. It was night outside. In an adjacent room, someone coughed to the point of hacking up something unpleasant.

Across the room sat an elderly man wearing an old-fashioned, pre-Revolution wig. The rest of his attire hearkened back a few decades. His bony countenance studied Trestan like a dead spider in a sugar bowl. Small pox scars covered his cheeks.

"Do you know where Henriette Sontag took those fragments of the Tenth?" the old man asked. His pleasant, conversational voice was at odds with his cold visage.

"I assume that is the only reason I am alive?" Trestan could still taste the sands of Serapis. Could still taste Ulrika's lips.

"Answer him." Fouché aimed the curved gun.

Trestan smiled. "You expect me to divulge secrets in the presence of this traitor?" He nodded at Fouché, whose face reddened.

The old man smiled thinly. "All spies are traitors, Trestan Desaix. Especially you. Salamanca, was it? Would that I had lived to see Napoleon's fall, rather than in these streams I now inhabit. But you aided your enemies, stole from your friends, and thus murdered your future. Do not assume gentlemanly airs."

"A gentleman introduces himself prior to engaging in intimate conversation," Trestan said in a nonchalant tone.

Fouché glowered. "Insolent cur—"

The old man held up a hand. "I am Joseph Haydn."

It was spoken with the weight and assumption that Trestan would know the man—which he did, by reputation. The prolific mentor of Mozart and Beethoven, Haydn had composed over a hundred symphonies. The darling of Europe's music theatres.

Trestan glanced at the open bedroom door, where the coughing continued. Hayden followed his gaze and nodded.

"This night will be his last. And do you know why?" Haydn chuckled as if telling a joke. "He refused us. He refused the very ones who instructed him in the intricacies of metaphonics. Do you know how much I did in the shadows of society, so that prodigy would receive the right attention? The best patrons? Yet he swilled it away like a drunkard gulps cheap wine."

Eying the manuscripts on the floor, one made Trestan stiffen. It was an aria from *Die Zauberflöte*… The Magic Flute.

Trestan scowled. "You are the murderers of Mozart."

The coughing increased, and an impassioned groan from the bedroom stung Trestan. He'd never been one for enjoying misery. That was why he'd chosen to be a spy, rather than fight on the front lines. But now, they were forcing him to fight anyway.

"Murderers?" Haydn shook his head. "Such a heavy, awful word. No, I am his deliverer. *Gott Lied* must ensure that only the Creator is allowed to change the universe, and that only Christ should walk on water—or through time. Mozart refused us. Thus he dies, to save his soul."

"Yet you walk through time," Trestan said. "You're trapped in it!"

Fouché cuffed him across the brow with the gun, and Trestan swooned. Blood ran down the side of his face, colors filled his sight.

Haydn examined his fingernails. "I am the guardian of the Creator's secrets. That is the duty of all the faithful. The Chorale was supposed to show people the path to righteousness, not become false gods, performing witchcraft and calling it science."

"By allying with this corpse?" Trestan glared at Fouché, who struck him again. Trestan slammed onto the floor, his blood-filled spittle staining Mozart's compositions.

"Even the dead can support our cause." Haydn paced the room, his steps rattling through discarded manuscripts. So many wonderful compositions, trodden upon. Mozart coughed louder and cried out. "Now…where did Henriette take those fragments?"

"I don't know," Trestan said.

Haydn held up Berlioz's wand. "The man who wielded this knew. But that stupid Russian shot him. That is another part of this predicament that Beethoven threw us into. He was willing to give metaphonics to whomever could unlock it. Now every composer, knowingly or not, is trying to complete what my former student perfected. What that dying man in that bedroom helped start."

Mozart gagged. The swish of sheets and the fall of paper scrolls filled the room.

Haydn nodded, and Fouché forced Trestan up and into the bedroom. Inside, a sickly young man writhed in sweaty sheets, a quill pen in one hand, an unfinished composition in the other. Drool slid from his slackened mouth.

"Why show me this?" Trestan asked. "Why make him suffer?"

"Because I loved him like my own son." Haydn gently squeezed Mozart's trembling hand. "Yet I am willing to sacrifice him, like Isaac on the mount, offered to the Creator. Mankind has reached too far. You will help restore us to our rightful place."

"The poison is done." Fouché studied a device with glowing red numbers.

"I…" Haydn released Mozart's hand. His jaw quivered. "Yes."

After a few jerky movements, Mozart ceased his struggles. A hollow, rattling sound rose in his chest, and escaped his lips. The tip of his quill leaked ink across the unfinished measure in dark Stygian lines.

"Goodbye, my friend." Haydn left the bedroom. Fouché forced Trestan to follow.

"Such cruelty…" Trestan glared at them.

Haydn snorted. "A Frenchman, lecturing me on cruelty? How quaint. I assume then, that you remain ignorant of Henriette's cruelties."

"I thought Ulrika worked for *Gott Lied*," Trestan said. Though he'd only suspected, he needed to feign knowledge to gain it.

"She did. But then again, do women ever serve anyone but themselves?" Haydn flung his arm out in dismissal. "She could be anywhere in space and time. I suspected she would come here, but she is crafty. Some dissenters, like her, believed that if Mozart were saved, then metaphonics would have flourished. That we would not have needed Beethoven, who proved to be less than an ideal comrade."

"His genius far exceeds yours," Trestan said.

Haydn's face hardened. "It most certainly did. I composed over a hundred symphonies, each unlocking another aspect of metaphonics so that we could better understand God's intent. But Beethoven reached the very stars with his nine symphonies. Less than a tenth of my output! And therein lies the tragedy. What could he have accomplished, had he not rebelled against the Chorale? Against God?"

"Rebelled?" Trestan asked as Fouché directed him to another room—one with a black cloak, bicorne hat, and a familiar black mask hanging from a coat rack.

"He was a revolutionary to the end," Haydn said. "Oh, what a fool I was, thinking he would change! He helped us defeat Napoleon, yes. Then he wanted to usurp the whole societal order, and that, we could not allow. Thus his final creation must remain hidden."

Fouché waved the curved gun. "Put on those garments and the mask."

Trestan snorted. "I am to become your hound, then? Sniffing her out?"

"I am confident your nose is already keyed to her scent," Haydn said. "She is quite beautiful. A great soprano. Yet she must die."

"What's in it for me?" Trestan asked, stalling.

"Spies do not bargain, they steal," Haydn said. "So steal back those fragments, and *Gott Lied* might intercede on your behalf to regain the Creator's forgiveness."

"If I refuse?" Trestan asked.

"You cannot refuse the future." Haydn waved Berlioz's wand. Temporal ripples emanated from it. The room around them transformed from a vestibule in late eighteenth century Vienna, to a metal and glass chamber hung with rectangular, glowing images. Steel arms driven by pistons and gears now held the jacket, hat, and mask.

Other men waited in line to receive similar accoutrements. The steel arms pasted and sealed the items directly to the subject's flesh. The glowing rectangles displayed their heartbeat, their body temperature, and cellular decay.

"I will resist." Trestan reached for either his tuner or the chime. Both were gone.

"That was what Beethoven said, before we loosed the skin beetles in his home," Haydn said. "They slowly devoured his eardrums while he slept. Each night, they gnawed away at his most treasured sense. Each morning, he was less of a man."

"Yet he persevered," Trestan said.

Fouché smiled. "As will you. For despite the pain, you will lead us to her—and what she has stolen." He shoved Trestan's tuner into Trestan's chest. The tines broke the skin, sending a pulse into his very bones.

Trestan reached for Fouché's throat as the steel arms enveloped him. The garments bonded to his flesh with searing pain. He fell to his knees, trying to pull them off. Haydn and Fouché watched with detached impatience. Finally, the mask sealed over his face, and Trestan screamed. He was now a specter of the dead genius.

A large resonator lowered from the ceiling. Haydn waved the wand, and both devices homed in to a specific vibration in space-time. A specific time. Trestan sensed it with the tuner, now permanently implanted into his chest.

"I will fight you all—!"

He found a discarded jumpsuit atop the next dune. It was weak, rotten. Like it had lain there for years. He kept going, leaving a crimson trail in his wake.

Trestan landed on a hard, compact surface. He was assaulted by a terrible cold.

Haydn walked over the dune, studying Berlioz's wand as if it were the greatest curiosity. "I find it entertaining, sending one of you godless Frenchmen to do the Creator's work. I recall when that diminutive piece of offal took the Vatican, and deposed the Pope for his Empire. I wanted to strangle him with my rosary that very night."

"You think you are of God?" As Trestan clasped the jumpsuit, the pain in his heart bothered him. He needed to find her more for himself, than for his enemies.

Chuckling, Haydn knelt on one knee. "I have asked myself that question countless times. Whenever I composed a new piece, I counted the rosary and prayed. Each time, I received His inspiration. I did not let that swell my ego."

"You lie." Trestan crawled up the dune. "Your arrogance cripples humanity."

Haydn watched Trestan struggle with infinite patience. "Do you know what separates us? Not language, or loyalty. Not even age. I am humble before the powers of Creation. Fools like you want to master them, to use them for your own pleasures and designs. Has not the Creator provided the designs already? You are greedy, and amoral. You hate God, while being jealous of him. You seek to take his place. Denial of his existence provides the emotional barrier you need to perform such a ghastly task."

Trestan laughed and staggered back. "You are lying to yourself. The quest of humanity has always been to become God. We make up pantheons, we write down laws in scripture. We build temples and sacrifice lambs, swords, or gold. In the end, we all want to exalt ourselves over that to which we were born. To master our reality."

Haydn rose in a huff. "You are beyond pity. Beyond hope, were it my say!"

"That is the true spirit of the Revolution, you sanctimonious bastard." Trestan stared at Haydn with a conviction he'd not felt in years. "To rise above those who would cast us into Hell, to take Heaven, whether it be by words, by a kiss, or by the sword."

"Blasphemy." Haydn squeezed the wand. "You create your own Hells, then inflict them on others. Look at what Napoleon brought about, and his intentions began as benevolence. Mankind cannot control itself!"

"Neither can your Creator!" Trestan cried. "We created God simply as a goal to overcome, a primitive edifice to tear down on our path to illumination!"

Haydn struck Trestan with the wand. It snapped, crumbling to silvery powder.

"There is your path, cretin. Your artifices turned to dust, while you wander in this extraterrestrial Sinai. Forty years Moses led them in the wilderness; forty years, I too, have now led the Gott Lied. The Promised Land is near. You will help me enter it."

Haydn pulled the silver chime and activated it. A sound carried around Serapis, disturbing the sand. Shaking it from dunes to reveal more ruins, more battlefields.

"You are already dead in my time." Trestan rose and faced him. "Whatever you did to Ulrika, whatever Talleyrand did to Fouché, you did to yourself. You are trapped between eras. Has it been worth it?"

Sadness filled Haydn's gaze. "We fool ourselves into thinking we control our destinies. The Chorale, even more so. Even I did, once. That is why you hurt so much inside, Trestan Desaix. You refuse to accept that you cannot change fate."

The sound increased in volume until Trestan had to flee. The air vibrated with the sheer force of the noise, and in the distance, the two columns were about to topple over. The ground quaked, knocking Trestan prone before reaching the columns.

He glimpsed her over the next dune. She clasped something to her chest.

"Ulrika!" His voice echoed off of flat, metallic surfaces.

He tried to duck as another boy threw a rock at him. It was nearing sundown. He'd been crucified that morning, and much to the Roman soldiers' disappointment, the vultures had let him be. The stone struck his collar bone with a pop, and he gritted his teeth against the pain. The little boy laughed and searched for another rock.

"You were warned about maintaining your focus," Talleyrand said, wearing a legate's cuirass and red cape. "You must concentrate. The vibrations are part of nature. We can bend light. We can shatter the atom. That is how you must approach this, Trestan. Now hurry. That boy just found a rather large stone."

"You fool!" Trestan yelled. "Fouché betrayed us! He's working for Gott Lied!"

"You think I do not know my allies, my enemies?" Talleyrand smiled, shading his eyes from the Levantine sun. "You are so close. Remember why you are doing this. Remember your country, your fallen emperor. The Revolution."

The boy tossed the stone. It slammed into the side of Trestan's cross. It made the spikes in his hands and feet vibrate. He gasped with agony.

"Focus on what you want," Talleyrand said. "Where you want to be."

Trestan thought about how much he needed to find Ulrika, to warn her. To protect her. How much he wanted to wring Fouché's neck, how much he'd love to smother Haydn in the sands of Serapis.

The boy laughed again. He found a third rock. Bigger, more jagged.

"Ulrika?" His voice echoed back to him as if he spoke inside a giant tube.

Trestan focused on what he had told Haydn back on Serapis, of how the Revolution was meant to benefit humanity. To lift it up from the depths of superstition, ignorance, and hatred and make the world anew. It was a pompous philosophy, grand and arrogant. But it epitomized who he was. When the soldiers killed those Spaniards, that had not been the true Revolution. When he had given false reports that brought about defeat at Salamanca, that, too, had not been the Revolution.

The cross shook.

He started to say her name again, but the mask deformed his words, stifled his breath. He touched it, withdrew his hands. It was like touching the face of a dead man. Maybe it was his true face, then, and not a mask.

The boy lifted the stone and sneered.

The cross shuddered. Trestan raised his head to the sky.

"Focus," Talleyrand said, then vanished.

Soon, the entire cross wobbled. The boy gaped at him and ran.

8.

Moderato in C major, Opus 31
Hesperus IV

The walls around him were typical Class II bulkheads, insulated from extrasolar radiation and microscopic particles. He lay on an octagonal dais surrounded by several large viewports. Green lights glowed from metallic consoles, showing all systems at 100%. The scent of scorched metal made his nostrils tingle.

Calculations flowed and resolved in his thoughts as the tuner pulsed in his chest.

[Gravity: 0.92 Earths. Atmosphere: nonexistent. Temperature: 272 kelvin.]

And he knew what all of that meant.

Trestan stared around at the starship's interior. It unnerved him, knowing the name and function of such technology. Whatever *Gott Lied* had done to him, they'd prepared him for this new era. It was all normalized, integrated into his mind. The tuner was now a temporal foci, a vibration sensor, a ripple initiator, and a database, all in one. His former self would have regarded it as magic. Now it was mundane.

The wonder of it still took his breath.

Outside the viewports was starry darkness. Though walls and glass were all that separated him from the vacuum, ambition was all that separated him from those distant suns, calculated in integers beyond human ken.

Fouché's mention of ships traversing the aether between worlds made him remember why he'd been sent here.

"Crew?" Trestan asked his embedded computer.

[34 Assigned; 34 Unaccounted for.]

He hesitated, then cleared his throat. "Henriette Sontag?"

[Not present on manifest.]

"Ulrika?"

[Not present on manifest.]

Teeth gritted, Trestan examined the garments melded to his body. His nerves still stung from the merger. Now, instead of just the cloak, hat, and mask, his hands were coated in black gloves, and thick boots protected his feet. Sleek material hugged his frame in a jumpsuit resembling the one Ulrika wore. Haydn had prepared him well.

The tuner shook, detecting a vibration nearby.

He left the octagonal chamber and entered a long corridor. Orange caution lights flashed on the ceiling. Nausea plagued him at times, and his steps lightened at certain bends in the corridor. Once, he even floated off the floor an inch or two.

[Normalizing environmental controls after recent breach.]

The tuner pulsed faster. Trestan followed the vibration, growing excited.

The next corridor, though, doused his enthusiasm.

Several bodies lay in pools of their own blood. Humans, in a gray uniforms bearing the Iron Cross of Germany. A few wore a red armband, featuring a black symbol inside a white circle. Among the corpses lay guns with small metal stocks and perforated barrels. Smoke drifted from the weapons. Bullet holes marred the floor and walls.

[Waffen SS. Armament: MP40 and MP28 submachine guns. Threat level: 0.]

"Who did they fight? Who won?" Trestan's voice echoed down the corridor.

[Unobtainable.]

Trestan stepped gingerly between blood and bodies until he entered another octagonal chamber. More dead lay within it; all of them in the same uniforms.

[Nazi Wehrmacht, circa 1945. Threat level: 0.]

"What did they want?" he asked.

[Unobtainable.]

The orange caution lights turned yellow. Trestan stared all around.

[Initiating docking procedure with Hesperus IV. Please remain buckled and ensure that all items are secured.]

A sinking feeling hit Trestan's stomach. His feet drifted off the floor again, but this time, he remained afloat. Bodies rose from the floor, frozen in death's embrace. Corpses, weapons, and shrapnel floated around Trestan. Whenever something bumped into him, it drifted in the opposite direction.

He pushed himself to a viewport. Outside, an asteroid hovered into view, backlit by green and purple nebula. Dark, cloud-like shapes obstructed some stars, while in other places, great clusters shone like a handful of diamonds on velvet.

The tuner vibrated, and Trestan followed the direction it indicated. He finally reached the airlock. The asteroid, large enough to hold a small city, was oval in shape, and pitted with deep craters. Again, it bothered him to automatically know what something was that he'd never seen before. It questioned his sanity, cheated his freewill.

The tuner urged him on.

A figure hurried over the asteroid, toward a grouping of metallic monoliths set into its surface. More bodies floated outside. Some wore the same Nazi uniform, but breath masks covered their faces. These corpses were stiff and covered in light frost. It took him a moment to realize the floating red droplets was blood.

A few robotic cuirassiers, the automatons he'd first met in Vienna, also drifted in the void. They numbered fewer, but had inflicted far more casualties. Perhaps this was their last stand. His tuner told him their systems were disabled.

The vessel shook, and with frightening suddenness, Trestan fell to the floor. The corpses and weapons slammed into the hard-plated deck.

[Now docked with asteroid Hesperus IV.]

The airlock opened, and atmosphere blew out. Trestan, bodies, guns, shrapnel—all was sucked out into the darkness. Flailing madly, he bumped into the corpses and grabbed at his mask. He still breathed.

[Oxygen at 88%.]

Though space was even colder, and he felt no resistance against his limbs, Trestan calmed down. The Chorale had already mastered this future. So would he.

The jumble of activity thrust Trestan toward Hesperus IV. It was even more impressive up close, with craters a pod of sperm whales could reside in. Several corpses struck it, the impact causing dust, pebbles, and small ice chunks to break off and float away into eternal nothingness.

When Trestan came within a few yards of the asteroid, an unseen force drew him rapidly to it. As soon as he touched down, blue lights lit along a paved causeway. His boots gripped the surface, and he walked without floating into the void.

Beyond the asteroid and the starship was a dull brown gas giant. The tuner relayed information to Trestan's brain: Hesperus I-III orbited the planet, once part of the same moon. The Chorale had broken it apart to disrupt time streams leading to this location. Such desperation could only mean one thing: part of the Tenth was here.

He reached the lip of a crater where an empty symphony awaited its performers. Metal stands affixed with screens, with a musical instrument floating before each. But these were unlike any items Trestan had ever seen. Violins with a dozen strings, trumpets with three bells, and flutes with more holes than two hands could manipulate.

In the center stood a single figure attired in black. He barely spotted them against the immense backdrop, like a shard of ebony against a night sky.

The vibrations emitted from the figure.

"Why?" His question carried on several frequencies, forever traveling the cosmos.

The masked figure turned. Beethoven facing himself at the edge of the universe.

"I had to," Ulrika said.

Trestan crossed over the lip of the crater and into the symphony pit. The dust of a thousand millenniums was disturbed by his steps. He knew their vibrations would be detected by Fouché, Talleyrand, or Maryshka. Yet the dreams of such men were still earthly ones; their greed of a simpler, mortal quality. These sights went far beyond anything Haydn gave humanity credit for. It proved that anything was possible.

"We've both been used by the enemies of progress," Trestan said. "I forgive your betrayal on Eurytion—"

"Forgiveness?" She laughed with scorn. "You're worse than Haydn. Liars such as we cannot offer it."

"And Berlioz?"

Ulrika's jaw tightened as she ran a gloved hand over a cello with four sound holes. Her thumb plucked one of the strings, and the vibration rung through Trestan. The tuner recited data to his mind: how the vibration keyed in to different time streams, how this location took advantage of gravitational qualities benefitting metaphonics.

"You asked for his help, and now he is dead," Trestan said. "His vibration wasn't like yours, immune to…"

"I've been blamed by countless men over time," she said. "You are no different."

He started to argue, then took a deep breath. His own mother was nearly executed for crimes against the Republic, in the years before Napoleon's rule. The Revolution had used, then shut out, women of strength and ideas.

"I cannot carry the guilt of the world," Trestan finally said. "Only my own."

"Our world is one of those small points above us." Ulrika caressed the cello. "There is only one way back to it from this location."

Trestan glanced at the starship.

"That vessel does not travel the streams," she said.

"These others could," Trestan said. "They were waiting for you?"

He pointed at the floating corpses, just now cresting over the crater, ruining the magnificent view with their reminder of cruelty and mortality.

"I shortened their wait." She accessed a piano with a keyboard totaling nine octaves. After playing a series of notes—the melody from Beethoven's Seventh Symphony, 2nd Movement—an invisible field formed over the orchestra pit. Trestan knew it only because of his tuner. Two robots powered back on, but they were damaged beyond any capacity for combat. She'd used the Chorale's defenses to gain more time.

[Artificial atmosphere detected. Status: 1%.]

"Ulrika … who are you waiting for?"

She aimed a curved gun at him, much like the one Fouché used on Maryshka.

[Armament: phase shifter, model 8.8. Threat level: 2.]

"What do they want with the Tenth?" Trestan risked another step. "The same thing that my superiors want? Don't give it to them."

"I've already found the fragment here," Ulrika said. "You shouldgo."

[Atmosphere status: 55%.]

"Do you know what they will do with it?"

"The same thing any being does with power." Ulrika swallowed. "Trestan … go!"

"Then shoot," Trestan said. "I did not come here for *Armée de L'ombre.*"

"You did not come here for me." Ulrika played more notes, unbinding the mask from her face. It floated away, a ghost without a haunt.

"I came for both of us." Trestan removed his own mask with little concentration. The power of the notes, the complexity of the formula therein, released it from his flesh.

They stared at each other, sucking in starving breaths.

[Atmosphere status: 70%.]

"You are a stubborn fool," she breathed.

He focused on the orchestra, and the instruments came to attention like a battalion of soldiers. Multiple destinations went through his mind as his tuner pulsated. He comprehended metaphonics on a greater level, not letting his thoughts shift. Imitating Berlioz, he was able to elicit a flurry of notes from the orchestra. Their vibration revealed his place in the current time stream, and Ulrika's. Hers was weak.

"Do not play with forces you think you understand," Ulrika said.

"Help me understand." Trestan walked up right beside her.

[Atmosphere status: 89%.]

"You are deaf to the streams, yet think you control them." She laid a hand on his chest. "With wisdom comes pain. Comes sacrifice."

"If what you wanted from me wasn't real … then make that sacrifice." Trestan gently removed the gun from her grasp. She backed into the piano keys, her rump creating a mashup of notes. Their vibrations emboldened him. He felt the same coming from her, a different vibration now singing in his heart.

"Let me help you." He concentrated, trying to combine them. "I can undo what—"

"You will not be the same after this," she whispered.

Their combined vibration spread, manipulating the instruments around them. The melody deepened, expanding into something overtaking the entire asteroid. Trestan held her unique stream in his mind. Viewing her life, exulting her triumphs, suffering her tragedies. His own unique stream flared. Moments from his past came and went, but he ignored them, drawing every vibration from his life into the current one. Unless his vibration was as strong as hers, he'd fail. Fail to give her a life again.

Ulrika shook in his arms. He focused harder, refusing to capitulate.

Yet, as the melody continued, the stream weakened. Her memories became illusion, her place in time, mere legend. His own stream faded in and out of space-time. Stars shimmered outside the dome, as if viewed from the bottom of a pool.

And Trestan was drowning at the bottom of it.

"Ulrika…?"

The vibration broke away, and Trestan collapsed atop the piano. She watched him with shame and pity. Both fueled his anger.

"What have you done?" he asked.

"I told you … this is what I chose."

The orchestra ceased its performance, and the final notes vibrated the very structure of the asteroid. The center of the crater opened up, and a metallic cylinder floated out. Ulrika grasped it and closed her eyes.

She'd used him, yet again.

"Are they worth it?" Trestan managed to stand. "Do you trust them with such power, the people you're giving it to?"

Ulrika gave him a sad look. "Goodbye, Trestan."

"Are they worth it?" Trestan yelled.

Trestan lay on the ground before the cross, hands and feet bleeding. The boy had ran into the village, where the soldiers waited. He needed to rise before they returned.

Ulrika sang a series of notes and activated her oscillator. A version of her appeared at each instrument, then faded from sight. She was gone, and he was alone on the lifeless rock.

MOVEMENT III

9.

Vivace in G minor, Opus 31
Early 1st century A.D.
Galilee

Trestan rose and stared at the cross, sensing vibrations coming from it. One of the spikes driven into his hand was actually a tuning fork. He pried it from the wood. It resembled the tuning fork he'd found in Beethoven's apartment.

According to his implanted tuner, it was an exact match.

Trestan swooned. Not only from the hot sun and loss of blood, but the questions boiling in his brain. How long had he been on this quest for Talleyrand? How many times had he comes this way? Was he the arsonist who'd destroyed Beethoven's home?

He couldn't explain why his own tuning fork had laid among the ashes.

Remembering the cruel boy and Roman soldiers, Trestan scampered behind a nearby house. The sun blistered his flesh without mercy while he counted seconds, then minutes. Still no sign of anyone. His tuner checked for any disturbances in the surrounding time streams. Nothing.

And yet...

Trestan swallowed with a parched throat and slowly stood.

A familiar vibration rippled just beneath the veneer of his current reality.

Barefoot, naked, hands and feet punctured, Trestan stumbled through the village. Using his old tactics, he avoided anyone's notice. He could stride across the time streams, but something made him physically navigate the mudbrick maze. Perhaps he needed a reminder that he was yet flesh and blood. It was the only thing *Gott Lied* hadn't stolen.

Finally, he came within sight of a grand stone palace. Its Hellenistic architecture hearkened back to Ptolemaic sensibilities, with columns and friezes. The structure bustled with servants and guests. Judean guards manned the battlements.

He really was in ancient Palestine.

The strains of an orchestra made him hurry up to the palace gates. He sneaked into a wagon filled with amphorae. Wine sloshed in each clay container. The temptation to slake his thirst made Trestan bite his fist to remain quiet.

Soon, the wagon was granted entrance. Trestan slipped further into the palace.

Now, the tuner was fully aligned with his consciousness. Between the vibrations of people, objects, and events, outside the current time stream—outside of time—his wounds didn't hurt. His skin was alleviated of its raging sunburn, and his thirst, nonexistent. Yet the anger within him burned even hotter, forming its own vibration.

Ulrika would not get the better of him again.

The deeper his infiltration, the louder the music became. It was piece he'd heard snippets from—snippets hummed by Ulrika. A temporal chanteuse, luring him into another trap. Or so she thought.

As he walked up stone steps into the keep, Trestan wondered who had crucified him. Wondered where Fouché could be. Wondered what part he was supposed to play. Trestan had no illusions about his own freewill in these matters now. But he would change that. He was the Revolution now, and Beethoven's Tenth would solidify that.

The sounds of a raucous party drifted from inside. Joyful voices rose above the orchestra music. Trestan scented roasted goat meat, the strong Nabatean wine reserved for nobility. He understand every voice, whether Greek, Latin, or Aramaic. Metaphonics granted him the ear of a polyglot.

He slipped past guests in silken robes, glutting themselves on the bountiful offerings of Herod Antipater, grandson of Herod the Great. Heroic bronze statues and caryatid columns advertised that these people still considered themselves heirs to Alexander's old empire. To them, the Romans were but a nuisance, and the Hebrews, a pestilence. The music swelled, echoing off the masonry walls, sloshing wine in numerous goblets. The affair bore similarities to events in his own time. The wealthy and powerful, sating themselves on the fruits of other's labors. He'd partaken of them himself many times, carrying out a mission. What a hypocrite he'd been.

He entered an atrium where the orchestra played: all were dressed in the uniforms of Imperial French infantry, complete with bearskin caps. The court, swaying with the music, seemed not to notice the strangers out of time. Fouché watched from a corner, nibbling on an orange, dressed as a Roman centurion. Atop a gilded throne, Herod laughed and clapped as a slight figure twirled in the center of the atrium, her bare feet perfectly balancing her on a mosaic of the god Pan.

Salome whipped a translucent veil about, teasing the audience with glimpses of flesh, tossing her black hair. Bracelets adorned her ankles and wrists, each worth a king's ransom. Kohl rimmed her eyes, darkened her lips—a chthonic Muse seducing him into the Underworld. Despite himself, Trestan was mesmerized by her complete command of her body. Salome was in control of everyone in the room, and she knew it.

Except for Ulrika, who stood beside Herod's wife, Herodias. They watched Salome with detached amusement. Ulrika was dressed like a Roman noblewoman, hair beset with pearls, shells, and lapis lazuli. A deep red *stola* draped her figure.

Trestan stood behind a column, avoiding Fouché's shark-like glance. He counted the number of guards, noted their weapons.

Though in no shape for confrontation, he had to try something. With Ulrika and Fouché both here, he wasn't going anywhere.

Gradually sidling up beside the throne dais, Trestan read Ulrika's and Herodias's lips. The skill had served him well at many other noisy parties in his career.

"Your husband will make war against Aretas of Nabatea, but the Romans won't support him," Ulrika said, close to Herodias's ear. "Afterward, the new emperor, Caligula, will exile you and your husband to Gaul. I cannot change that."

Herodias paled. "And my daughter?" She indicated Salome.

"I will ensure she weds her stepfather's son," Ulrika said. "She'll bear three children, living long and in comfort."

Herodias finally clasped Ulrika's hand. "Then you shall have what you ask."

The music swelled on the strings, and Salome flung away the veil. Herod ogled her like a meal he was ready to eat. The scene's debauchery upset Trestan, who still despised monarchial abuse of power. He turned away—finding Ulrika's stare upon him.

There was nothing left but the smokestacks of buildings. All was rubble, ash, and the smoldering embers of spent aggression. The distant clank and roll of tank tracks was a reminder that the killing machines were never far away, that one of them could incinerate Trestan in an instant. He scowled at the Mauser in his hands, then dropped it.

[Soviet T-34 tanks, 7th Guards Tank Corps. Threat level: 3.]

"I warned you about shifting, you goddamn fool," Fouché whispered in his ear.

Trestan was once again watching Ulrika from across the dais, and he hated himself for desiring her. Yet his ideals couldn't supplant the emotions she summoned within him. Her painted fingernails emitted a pearlescent gleam, making her seem like Tiamat, risen from the sea to entice humanity once more.

Herod abandoned his throne and paced around the atrium, drawing ever closer to Salome. Trestan balled his fists, but Fouché stuck something cold and hard into his back.

[Armament: phase shifter, model 9.0. Threat level: 3.]

"And here I assumed spies were heartless tools," Fouché said. "You played against her, and lost. Now remain still, and we might salvage this situation."

"To whose gain?" Trestan muttered over his shoulder.

The implanted tuner detected vibrations across the ruins of Berlin. Resistance had ended. All that remained were the smiling victors, the cries of the violated, and the smoldering corpses of old men and boys.

"Focus!" Fouché said in a fierce whisper. "Else you will trap us in one of those places you keep returning to."

Returning to? Trestan went cold. His thoughts, his recollections—these 'shifts' in space-time—were actually memories of when he'd visited those places. The implications froze his very being. He was trapped in an eternal cycle.

Trapped between the vibrations of time, like Ulrika had warned him.

"What do you want me to do?" he finally asked, still watching Ulrika.

"When this ignorant potentate offers her the gift—you must kill Ulrika."

He was a spy. A man of intrigue, a liar stealing through another's house in the middle of the night, a false witness to fallen emperors. He wasn't a murderer.

There weren't enough wagons to cart off the French dead at Salamanca; by midday, vultures had solved that problem. Soon, the arid air of the Spanish afternoon bloated the bodies. Trestan smelled the stench long after he'd ridden down the road.

He was a murderer. Of men and ideas. Of hope.

"Then give me a weapon." Trestan swallowed.

Salome knelt with hands upraised, her performance finished. The court cheered and clapped as the final notes of Richard Strauss's *Salome* faded away.

Herod held up the veil and sniffed it. "What gift could I possibly grant to such a feat? You may ask anything, even unto the half of my kingdom."

Herodias looked up in surprise, and the courtiers fell silent.

Fouché tensed, then pressed a phase shifter into Trestan's hand.

Salome rose to her full height, as shameless as Aphrodite rising from her clam. Her jewelry glittered like stars. "Bring me the head of the Baptist."

Herod's joy faded, and the courtiers whispered among themselves. Herodias sat up straight. A slight smirk formed on Ulrika's face.

Across the city, Soviet soldiers placed their grand red flag atop the bullet-ridden Reichstag. It made a pitiable coda to such destruction.

"Proud of yourself?" Maryshka asked behind him. "I warned you…"

"Do it," Fouché whispered.

Trestan raised the gun. No doubt he'd used it before, in some other era.

After a grudging nod, Herod beckoned one of his servants. Moments later, the servant brought a dish covered with a silken cloth. Flies buzzed at its edges.

"Do it," Fouché said. "Fulfill your oath to the Revolution."

"You betrayed *Armée de L'ombre*," Trestan murmured. "I do not trust—"

"I am a double agent, imbecile. We waited until our enemies nearly destroyed each other, but his head was lost in the streams. Now do it."

Ulrika studied Trestan from the corner of her eye. There was no guilt there, nor malice. The weapon shook in his hand. He could kill her, take the Tenth for *Armée de L'ombre*. He could kill them all, claim it for himself. For the Revolution.

Herod lifted the cloth, revealing Haydn's head. The old composer's visage was one of pain and vexation. Roman *denarii* covered the eyes. Ready for a journey into Hell.

"Has it been worth it?" Maryshka raised his saber.

Haydn's once-proud features sank. "We fooled ourselves into thinking we control our destinies. That is why you hurt. You refuse to accept that you cannot change fate."

Trestan stood between the stone columns on Serapis, their vibration holding him in place while the pair faced off on a nearby dune. Dozens of Spetsnaz soldiers lay dead, their Kalashnikovs still smoking. Even more members of Gott Lied littered the desert, all wearing the countenance of Beethoven.

"I will make it quick," Maryshka said. "That is more than I can say for your future brethren, when I find them."

Try as he might, Trestan couldn't move. Caught between the streams at last.

"That harlot passed Beethoven's secrets to Wagner, and thus, to those who would raise the eagle standard once more." Haydn knelt. "God have mercy on us all."

Maryshka swung. The head stopped rolling at Trestan's feet.

"Quintilius Varus, give me back my legions," Trestan whispered.

"Now!" Fouché yelled.

The time stream shifted, and now, everyone noticed Trestan. The courtiers shrank back, and Herod shouted for his guards. Ulrika grabbed the head and ran.

Fouché aimed at her, but Trestan fired first. A fine yellow beam struck the old spymaster, and Fouché crumbled to the floor. A large hole smoked in his chest.

"The revolution is dead," Trestan said. "Long live the Revolution."

The French soldiers in the orchestra reached for their weapons, but Trestan shot two of them. The rest dashed for cover. Courtiers screamed and fled. Herod shouted for more guards, Salome's veil dangling in his fist.

Trestan ran right before the guards flung their spears. The missiles struck the wall. He chased Ulrika from the atrium, up a staircase. The entire palace was alerted, with guards scurrying over the grounds like ants on fire.

"Wait!" His steps left bloody footprints, and he had to stop twice. Ulrika was already atop a battlement. The coins in Haydn's head glimmered in the Judean sun.

"Why kill him? To what gain?" Trestan still couldn't move.

"Gain?" Maryshka lifted Haydn's head. "This will not happen again. I will find and destroy every fragment of the Tenth. But next, I will destroy your Shadow Army."

"I don't serve them anymore…" Trestan concentrated on his tuner, to no avail.

"Neither do you serve yourself." Maryshka thrust the saber at him.

"Ulrika!" He stumbled and fell on the battlement stairs. The wounds in his palms bled, staining the mudbrick red.

She looked back at him as she held up her oscillator. The next moment, twelve versions of herself scurried about the palace. The guards pursued the wrong ones.

This time, Trestan discerned the real Ulrika. The others were mere phantoms, translucent as ghosts. She stood on the battlement's precipice, the wind tossing her hair. He felt a complex series of vibrations emanating from her, and he realized she had implants as well. She raised her voice in a florid note. The vibrations increased.

Despite his wounds, Herod's guards, or his exhaustion, Trestan's mind stilled. The calculations of metaphonics translated from the tuner directly into his thoughts. He attuned to each vibration Ulrika summoned, each one she affected, from the current era to her next destination. The streams coursed around him, instead of against him.

The calculations possessed the power and nuance of emotions, feeling like a million different textures on his skin. He had become a sensate of space-time.

Forcing himself to move, Trestan fired the gun. The stones shattered beneath Ulrika's feet. She fell off the battlement just as he leapt from the staircase and caught her. Their vibrations intertwined as they plummeted into nonphysical space.

10.

Larghetto Tenerezza in G major, Opus 31
1150 A.D.
County Palatine of the Rhine

Trestan knelt between the stone columns on Serapis again. The stigmata he'd received, courtesy of Herod, was gone. He was still naked, but every time the windborne sand scratched his flesh, it healed over.

[Life functions restored to 100%.]

He lifted a handful of sand, then let it fall through his fingers. "Where am I?"

The tuner throbbed. [Serapis. Gateway world. Cellular repair default still active.]

Haydn had been wrong. The Chorale had chosen Serapis as a start and end point for all their journeys. Healing any damage they might have received with a shift in time, a rearrangement of atoms. The more he pondered it, the less complicated it was.

Resurrection, indeed.

The floor chilled Trestan's skin. A heavy, jingling garment weighed him down.

"You can't let the Church stop you." Ulrika's voice, muffled.

"There are those who say I am a heretic." Another woman's voice. "But I cannot help how I feel about … about him."

Trestan opened his eyes to slits. He lay in a room with stone walls. The women's voices came from behind a wooden door. Snowflakes floated in from a window.

"Don't stop," Ulrika said. "Your work will inspire many more than you know."

"With these melodies you have given me? Why, they are no different than I have already written! It is the words that matter, anyhow."

"Trust me," Ulrika said. "Let us try it, shall we?"

Ulrika and the woman lifted their voices in a gentle song of prophets, patriarchs, and virtues. Trestan recognized it from the tuner's database: it was the opening to Ordo Virtutum, Hildegard's most celebrated work. At least, in the centuries after Trestan's lifetime. Ulrika's soft yet powerful voice rose in melodious monotone, doubling Hildegard's vocal. Pure, firm, confident. The hymn of a believer who wanted to love her god in ways that would have horrified her superiors in the Church.

The vibration created by the song was familiar. Trestan's tuner checked and double-checked its database before reporting.

[Song contains trace elements of Beethoven's Tenth Symphony, as discovered on Eurytion. Undetectable to the human ear.]

Ulrika was spreading Beethoven's secret. Fulfilling Haydn's nightmare.

The cold air made Trestan's nose twitch.

"It does feel…different," Hildegard said in a joyful tone. "I shall add it to the other works our sisters will perform later. Bless you, child."

Trestan sneezed.

"Whoever could that be?" Hildegard asked. Someone started opening the door.

"Allow me, Prioress," Ulrika said. "It is probably one of the visiting pilgrims."

After Hildegard left, the door creaked open. Trestan shut his eyes. The door shut.

"You ignoramus!" A foot dug into his ribs. Coughing, Trestan opened his eyes.

Ulrika leaned against the stone windowsill, clutching Haydn's head. Now she wore the habit of a nun, but the fabrics were cruder, more austere. Instead of a rosary and crucifix, the oscillator dangled from a chain wrapped about her waist.

Trestan sat up on the cold stone floor. Though his wounds ached, they no longer bled. He wore a chain mail hauberk under a tunic emblazoned with the fleur-de-lis. His pants and boots were spattered with mud, as if from long travel. Realizing he held a sword in one hand, and the phase shifter in the other, he slowly stood.

"They wanted me to kill you," he said. "Tell me I made a wise decision."

"I'm tired of suffering men's decisions." Ulrika reached for the oscillator.

He aimed the gun. She went still.

"I want answers." When she didn't speak, he scowled. "Tell me, damn you!"

A knock came at the door. "Sister Ulrika? Is everything alright?"

Trestan discerned the older German dialect, like every other human language ever spoken, and yet to be spoken. But he'd lost the language of compromise. He had provided no return on *Gott Lied*'s investment, nor would he. Fouché was dead, and Trestan could never go back to Talleyrand and *Armée de L'ombre*. The quest was his own now.

"Everything is fine," Ulrika called. "I am simply consoling a French pilgrim."

The nun outside mumbled her apologies and left.

"You're no priest," he muttered.

"And your ideals offer absolution?" She tugged down her habit, releasing her rich brown locks. She could be Mary, Mother of God, such was her presence.

Such was her familiarity with every era he'd encountered her in.

"How many people have you aided through the centuries?" Trestan neared the window. The countryside below lay in the thrall of winter. Leafless tress, snowdrifts, smoke drifting from chimneys in the village. Its domesticity riled him.

"It is better to help, than to be a slave."

He pressed against her, the sword at her throat. "I'm not anyone's slave."

"Then whom do you serve?" She regarded him with scorn. "For you are not yet master of yourself."

Cheeks burning, he lowered the sword. "I serve a higher purpose."

"Truly." Ulrika set Haydn's head on the windowsill. "He thought the same."

He leaned closer. She stunk of altar incense and coarse soap. The fragrances of medieval captivity. She was like a bird in a cage, living atop the abbey in the tower. Trestan wasn't sure if he wanted to break her wings, or help her fly again.

"You asked for my help," he said. "You said we could do this together. I can change your stream, Ulrika. But you betrayed me!"

"That is what spies do." She stared outside as snowflakes floated past the window. "Stop pretending that you are honorable. That you really are a knight in shining armor, come to rescue me. You cannot even save yourself."

"I am a spy no longer." He grabbed her habit and tugged. "I killed Fouché. He wanted me to shoot you instead. Now I can't go back. They seek me, like they seek you. I have tied my fate to yours, whether you like it or not."

"I like it not," she whispered.

"To hell with it, then." He turned, breathing heavily.

"We bring hell with us, across these many heavens." She allowed snowflakes to fill her palm. "The mystic, the dreamer, the scientist—all search for the same thing. We are all the same archetype: lost in the past, despising the present, and thirsting for the future. But you and I, we despoil all three in our search." The snow melted in her palm.

"We can stop it." Trestan sat on the windowsill beside her. The chill air made him shiver inside his armor. "We can use them, instead of them using us."

"That makes us any better?" Ulrika sighed. "Sword, pistol, crucifix—men find it easier to make proclamations with steel in their hand."

Trestan tossed gun and sword to the floor. "What will it take to convince you?"

"Help me stop what is coming." She held up the oscillator.

"This must be torturous for you." He took her hand. "Needing a fool—"

"Like you," Wagner said. "They like you as Brünnhilde. I won't hear of anyone else performing this role!"

Ulrika, wearing a Valkyrie costume, shook her head. "You don't understand. The men coming don't care about this opera, they care about what you can do for them!"

Trestan, now attired as a Norse god, complete with winged helm, stared out over Eurytion's landscape. They stood beside the same orchestra pit where Berlioz perished, but the vegetation was shorter. On the mountain slope below, several robot units kept watch. There were no skeletons.

The battle hadn't taken place yet.

"I'll hear no more of it. Let's start with The Funeral of Siegfried again." Wagner adjusted his slouched beret cap and smoothed his silken jacket. The venerable composer was in the later stages of his life, wrinkled and squinting. Yet his energy was infectious, and his demand for perfection, emotionally crushing.

[Temporal anomaly detected.]

"Ulrika?" Trestan pointed at figures wending through the stone monuments below. Eurytion's sun made their rifles gleam.

[Waffen SS. Special Division. Threat level: 1.]

"I know." She hurried over to Wagner, who already had metaphonic control of the orchestra's instruments. They floated in place, warming up with a low hum. Its vibration hinted at the power about to be unleashed from Wagner's composition.

"Listen to me!" Ulrika cried.

"I am so glad you could come, fräulein!" Wagner grabbed Ulrika and kissed her cheeks, then flung her away and proceeded to gesticulate at the orchestra.

[Waffen SS. Special Division. Threat level: 2]

Trestan adjusted his phase shifter. The weapon's beam struck a target across multiple streams, guaranteeing death, even for individuals like

Ulrika or Fouché. He had no idea how Maryshka survived it. Or how they'd survive their current predicament.

"I can't make him understand, Trestan," Ulrika said. "This is how it happened last time. Damn his stubbornness!"

Hands raised, Wagner conducted the unearthly orchestra with aplomb and unfettered passion. His range of gestures were the envy of pantomimes, but the effect was anything but invisible. Eurytion quaked beneath them, and the planetary ring vibrated visibly. Megaliths lifted from the ground like saints ascending to Paradise. Each bore its own unique vibration, adding to the performance. The ensemble wracked Trestan's mind.

[Waffen SS. Special Division. Threat level: 3.]

Across the mountainside, the Chorale's robotic guardians engaged the Nazi soldiers. Though their blades and phase guns massacred platoon after Waffen platoon, the assault continued. Bullets shattered stones, mortars and grenades leveled trees. Robots exploded in fiery clouds. The fallen covered slopes, filled ravines.

Satan would not be kept from Eden.

"Trestan, help me!" Ulrika hovered like the Valkyrie she imitated. The music's power levitated robots and soldiers, boulders and groves. Wagner ascended into the air, still conducting. Focused on his own stream, Trestan barely resisted the music's pull.

"This is what he wanted," Wagner called. "This is what Beethoven meant!"

Trestan aimed and fired.

Ulrika stared across the courtyard as soldiers on horseback approached the abbey. They wore an inordinate amount of black. "They found us."

[Temporal anomalies detected.]

He didn't look out the window as the sound of galloping hooves came closer. Already he heard the ring of mailed bodies moving in leather saddles. Metaphonics informed him of all vibrations, all disturbances in the time stream. "You have the head of *Gott Lied*'s founder. I killed my immediate superior. But I would know who my ally is before we go any further."

She wrenched her hand away. "I never said we are allies."

The horsemen entered the courtyard, wearing black masks. Their leader stared up at the very window where Trestan and Ulrika argued.

"I tried to warn you," she whispered. "I told you that once you bind with the stream, you may never leave it. We are scattered across time, on different worlds."

"That's why you seek the Tenth," he said. "Not for them."

A nun screamed. Trestan looked down, glimpsed red snow, and grabbed the weapons. He took Ulrika's hand and kicked the door open. They ran from the room and down the tower steps. Fists pounded on the abbey door below. Nuns scurried everywhere.

"All that I do is for them!" Ulrika cried.

"Then run faster!" Trestan called.

An axe smashed into the abbey door. A nun's shriek was cut short.

[Thirty assailants. Combined threat level: 3.]

Trestan and Ulrika hurried into the inner courtyard. Nuns ran about, praying for aid, or reprimanding the *Gott Lied* even as the masked figures cut them down.

"There!" Ulrika pointed at a cistern.

The *Gott Lied* rushed into the inner courtyard, slaughtering any in their path. Trestan tried running faster, but the hauberk slowed him down. Ulrika gained on him, tossing off the nun's habit. Underneath she wore a dark blue jumpsuit.

Crossbow bolts whizzed past. Trestan reached the cistern as Ulrika activated her oscillator. A bolt knocked the sword from his grasp. Another thudded into his back. He fell over into the cistern, taking her with him. They spiraled into dark waters.

"Warned me?" Trestan turned and raised his hands as Maryshka aimed the submachinegun. "You hypocrite. You have used it, just as I have."

"Fight fire with fire." Maryshka stood atop a pile of rubble, his olive drab uniform far plainer than the one he'd worn at Borodino more than a century ago. But war in their current era had lost its pomp and nonsensical circumstance. Gone were the heroics of raised sabers and marshals leading charges. Now, peasants led the charges, straight into the fiery maws of machine guns,

tanks, and mortars. War had always been madness, but the one Trestan now witnessed would have given Napoleon nightmares.

"And burn the world down around us?" Trestan asked.

Maryshka watched T-34 tanks plow through a brick building, scattering enemy civilians that had been hiding. "The world burned down long ago, Frenchman. We have lived in its ashes since the time of Gilgamesh. We have created gods, murdered in their name, then slain those very deities. Sacrificed on the altar of your revolution."

"Your countrymen had their own revolution." Trestan glanced at the red flag waving over the skeletal skyline. "How many did Stalin starve? How many perished—"

"Do not lecture me." Maryshka cycled the submachinegun's chamber. "Glinka uncovered some of Beethoven's formulas, and passed them on to Mussorgsky. He in turn was driven mad, using metaphonics to send us to these strange worlds. But no more."

"We can end it." Trestan opened his left fist. In it was a fragment of manuscript.

"I have already ended it." Maryshka aimed at him. "Hands behind your head."

Trestan complied. The fragment blew away as La-7 fighter planes flew overhead.

"On your knees." Maryshka gazed at him with the pain of decades. He must have seen millions die in the many conflicts and tragedies since that fateful day in 1812.

Other Soviet troops forced German POWs to kneel in the debris-filled alley.

Again, Trestan obeyed. "This is how the Einsatzgruppen did it on the Eastern Front. Execution style."

Maryshka swallowed. "Not always. People were often shot where they stood, right next to the trenches where they could be buried together like dogs. Like dogs!"

"Then be a man." Trestan met his eyes. "Not a dog."

Maryshka's face crumbled for a moment, then he glared. "This is the only way."

"Help me end it," Trestan said. "No more genocides, no more war. The Tenth can help us understand one another. A real revolution, of the heart and mind."

Berlin was silent, as if it, too, could not believe the horrors were over. They both stared at each other, in the brick dust, smelling cordite and blood.

"You dream, my friend." Maryshka's voice was thick, and his shoulders shook.

The Soviets aimed at the baby-faced Hitler youth, the toothless old men.

"Don't do this!" Trestan cried.

Maryshka wiped his eyes. "It… it is too late. Too much has been done, too many have died. There is no hope for humanity. Not after this."

"There is only one fragment left," Trestan said. "I can—"

Maryshka fired. Three rounds punctured Trestan's body. He sucked in a breath and slumped over into the dust with the rest of the dead.

11.

Allegretto in D major, Opus 31
Thetis Prime

"Can you hear me?"

[Life functions at 28%. Temporal lag ongoing.]

Trestan clasped the bloody tuning fork as the Soviet tank came closer. Maryshka had already left, disappearing into the tomb that was Berlin. Bullet holes still smoldered in the bodies of the executed POWs. He should be dead, too. Again and again and...

[Gravity: 0.96 Earths. Atmosphere: Terraformed III. Temperature: 291 kelvin.]

Someone dragged him onto an atoll. The surface anemones scattered, their pink and green tentacles glowing in the light of Thetis Prime's gas giant neighbor, Thetis II. The planet functioned as a second sun at night, lighting the endless waves in mauve and teal shades. It would have been beautiful, if he didn't hurt like hell.

He clasped the tuning fork and focused on the vibration leading to the last world Beethoven found. Before Gott Lied destroyed most of his devices and shut him off from society. But Trestan had learned some of the late composer's tricks. The opening notes of Beethoven's Fifth Symphony gave his mind clarity.

Hands pressed down on his stomach, and Trestan vomited up water.

"I should leave you here to die," a frustrated voice said. "How I wish I could!"

The tank rumbled closer, rolling over bodies, fallen walls. The tuner told him which cracks were the sounds of crushed bones; which pops were the sounds of masonry bursting under the mechanized behemoth. Each throbbed in his chest, a vibration of life ending, and entropy continuing. Like he had continued, regardless of wounds suffered.

"I hate you." Palms slapped his chest. "Do you hear me? I hate you!"

Trestan gasped in pain.

Trestan squeezed the phase shifter's trigger. The Nazi about to shoot Wagner fell.

"Where are you taking us?" Trestan shielded the composer with his body as bullets darted at them from below. Yet higher and higher he, Ulrika, and Wagner rose, until they were well out of the Nazis' range.

"To the beginning, the prelude, the foundation... the overture." Wagner smiled.

Their streams shifted in space-time, and they were no longer on Eurytion.

[Life functions at 40%.]

"Oh no... what have I... oh no."

The T-34's treads came within inches of his leg as Trestan finally activated the tuning fork. One moment he was about to be crushed on the streets of Berlin, then he was lying on an atoll on another world, light years from Earth.

Light years away...

"Ulrika?" he managed, then moaned in agony.

Hair dripping, she leaned over him, wearing the jumpsuit she'd revealed in their flight from the abbey at Rupertsberg. Fear pinched her face, widened her eyes. She examined his chest and found three bullet holes—right before they vanished.

"You fool," she breathed. "You don't know what you've done."

"It was the only way to find you... by placing myself outside the streams."

Ulrika shook her head and gingerly toughed his chest. "You shouldn't..."

"I told you..." he took a ragged breath. "We're in this together."

"Goddamn you, Trestan." Ulrika kissed him. "I didn't want this..."

"Neither did I … until we danced to Berlioz's guitar." He touched her cheek.

While waves splashed at their feet, Trestan studied Thetis Prime's ever-shifting surface: an oceanic world, ninety percent water, the rest comprised of scattered atolls, islands, and volcanic outcroppings. Like other planets discovered by the Chorale, it bore unique gravitational alignments that were sensitive to metaphonics. Though smaller than Earth, it was just as beautiful, with a dizzying array of mollusks, crustaceans, and anemones. Cousins to those of his world.

Cousins. That was how he saw the human race now. He'd tried imparting that to Maryshka, and now, to Ulrika. Did she love him? The kiss was real, its vibrations coming from her heart and the neurotransmitters in her brain governing emotion …

Trestan ignored the rest of the tuner's data. Life still had meaning, despite what metaphonics had done to him. He longed for mystery, for only therein could humanity be saved: without it, there was no struggle to learn, to discover. Like the alien world around them, discovered by a deaf dreamer sitting before the keys of his piano.

"Who shot you?" she asked. "I sensed the vibrations from … my old homeland."

"Maryshka is hunting me through time." Trestan grunted in pain as his tuner uploaded the pertinent data into Ulrika's implants, detailing each encounter with the Russian. "We must hurry, before he comes here. And he will."

"Trestan …" Her voice broke with emotion.

By the time he turned back to her, Ulrika was gone. Her vibration, undetectable.

The next moment, two robotic cuirassiers walked down the atoll. They clanked to a stop beside Trestan.

"I don't under—" Trestan cried out as the robots picked him up.

[Life functions at 50%.]

"Why am I not healing? I passed through Serapis!"

[Unobtainable.]

Waves dashed against the rocky atoll while they approached a tetrahedron-like structure. It floated above the ocean, unsupported by any physical aids. Legless robotic cuirassiers hovered around, carrying phase shifters like the one he'd used on Fouché.

As they neared the shore, steps rose from the spume. They ascended above an ocean that would have been Nemo's dream. But that novel was before Trestan's current time. If he had a time any longer. A man of all eras, all worlds … yet a man of nothing.

"Where is Ulrika?" He glared at the robots.

[Unobtainable.]

At the staircase's apex, the robots deposited Trestan on a hovering stretcher. It carried him into the structure, and the beautiful scenery outside gave way to a familiar set of gardens. Familiar topiaries.

He was back at Château de Valençay.

"What is this?" He tried rising, but the robots held him prone on the stretcher.

The interior smelled the same; sex, wine, dust from generations of bureaucrats who'd ruled through secrecy. The robots stopped in a new room of the house, which featured a modern—in the relative sense of the term—medical facility. Automated surgeons replaced the tuner in his chest with a new one, and diagnostics were run on his blood, degrees of radioactive exposure, and cellular decay.

[Life functions at 100%. Temporal lag under control.]

"Ulrika?" he called.

"She has a head start on you." Talleyrand's voice, smug and calculating. "It is good to see you again, Trestan. You have traveled farther than any thought possible. Then, you achieved the impossible. I congratulate you."

Trestan blinked, and the next moment he stood in Talleyrand's sitting room. Attired in a uniform similar to Ulrika's, Trestan felt new. Too new, like a toy soldier with its gears replaced at a workshop.

Talleyrand stood behind a chair, holding a glass of wine. He had a little less hair, but more wrinkles and liver spots. Robot sentries watched from every corner.

"Ulrika works for you?" Trestan asked.

"She always did, my good man. I lured her from *Gott Lied* not long before Beethoven's death. That fool Haydn thought he could entice the younger generation with his silly religious zealotry. Songs of God, indeed."

On the mantle behind Talleyrand rested Haydn's head.

"Behold, the Baptist." Talleyrand chuckled. "Though it wasn't our allies that made him thus. That stupid Russian officer mutilated poor Haydn like this. But would you believe the old fool hid a fragment of the Tenth on his very skull? Amazing."

Trestan tried to keep his gaze neutral, even as he glanced everywhere for a weapon. "I killed Fouché. In that little shithole in Galilee."

Talleyrand grinned. "And you have my thanks. He was playing both sides for his own gain. I knew all along, but I wanted him close, so that I could discover his allies. He was a brute and a ghoul. I drink to the death of a dead man." He gulped the wine.

"So … do you have it all? The Tenth Symphony?"

"Of course not." Talleyrand set aside the empty glass and regarded Trestan flatly. "That is why I ordered you repaired at all cost. I apologize for the discomforts it will cause you, but we are nearly there. There is but one fragment left."

"And Ulrika?" Sweat rolled down Trestan's face.

"You are fond of her." Talleyrand stared out the windows at Thetis Prime's swells. "If not for Ulrika, your quest would have failed. Beethoven made it so that only two people, with a strong emotional attachment, would be able to unlock the Tenth's hiding places. Your personality profile matched Ulrika's. We knew you'd like her."

Trestan didn't hide his glare.

Talleyrand smiled. "You are right to be angry. Haydn accused you of wanting to become god, Fouché thought you a dumb tool, Berlioz placed unfounded hope in your revolutionary passion … but there was only one possible end to this. More lives than yours, more centuries than have been recorded, were put into this effort. It is not an evil one, Trestan. It is what must be."

"And what is that?" Trestan shook with anger. "More of the same? More war, more slavery, more poverty of the mind and of the larder?"

Talleyrand clasped something long and silken, studying it without seeing it. "Those are natural forces, keeping order. Like flame devouring old forest, or volcanoes reshaping the land. Like a tyrant reaping a harvest of fools, so that we have heroes, villains. We are nothing without them."

"We are the very engines of possibility!" Trestan cried, finding he couldn't move. He glanced at his arms and legs, looked at the robots. He was less human than the man standing before him, less human than those who'd slaughtered people on the Eastern Front... and he hated Talleyrand for it.

"Even your hatred of me, and your love for Ulrika." Talleyrand crushed the cloth in his fist. "That is what Beethoven did not understand. He tried to change what we are. The only thing we can be. Humans are imperfect. They cannot hope to aspire to the perfection the Chorale espoused. Only a few, with wisdom and intelligence, can know the secrets of metaphonics. It is not for the common man and woman, Trestan. Such a revolution would destroy itself, and thus, our species. I am saving us from ourselves."

"That's why they died?" Trestan's voice was filled with the anguish of a millennium. "That is why you killed Beethoven, Mozart, Schubert, and the Fates know how many others? You are traitors to progress, traitors to everything we live and die for!"

Talleyrand smirked. "Not all of us need die for it, though. That is why I am sending you to find the last piece of the Tenth. Either Wagner or that damned Russian has it, I am certain. Ulrika will lead you there, like always."

"You corrupted her!" Trestan was near tears in his fury. Furious that he couldn't move, that he was no longer his own person. If he ever had been.

"She wanted to be what she is now." Talleyrand tossed the cloth onto the table. "She too has seen what humans do with too much power. She made the mistake of giving that Teutonic hack a bit of the Tenth. His Valkyries heralded the destruction you think your Revolution can stop. Like you, she thinks her quest noble. And, like you, she is a means to an end."

Trestan eyed the cloth. He shook with impotent wrath.

It was Salome's veil from Herod's palace, lying beside a hammer and spikes.

Talleyrand smiled. "Ambition removes all inhibitions."

Trestan screamed his rage until Talleyrand stabbed him with the bloody tuning fork, paralyzing him. "Yes, I crucified you to lure Ulrika, my reluctant messiah. Now go back and be the devil. Find and burn Wagner, that Russian. You come full circle, now."

"Bastard," Trestan managed through gritted teeth.

"Be content that I allow you to remember what she felt like, tasted like. I owe you that much for your service."

The fork vibrated as he grabbed after Talleyrand. Château de Valençay shifted from sight. Bodies, buildings, empires, entire worlds flipped past him in an instant. He held his head in his hands, trying to control the stream, trying to make it stop. Yet his implants worked only for Talleyrand, like the tool he'd always feared himself to be.

And Ulrika....

His anger threw him across epochs, a terminal comet on course to collide with a future version of itself. A vicious circle he'd helped create, and could not escape.

Trestan appeared in Beethoven's sitting room. Vibrations spread from his tuner, disturbing matter at the atomic level. Creating friction, building heat. Flames spurted from shelves, chairs. The blaze spread quickly, becoming the tableau he'd first seen upon entering the apartment in 1827. Or had it been the first time?

He ran to and fro, trying to douse the growing blaze. His movements made him drop the bloody tuning fork. It clattered to the floor and emitted a sharp tone.

[Temporal lag accelerated.]

Somewhere, on distant worlds, the vibration activated numerous orchestras. They didn't require players or conductors, for that was Trestan himself. Accessing the Chorale's metaphonics network, its sheer power awed him. The musical instruments on Serapis, Eurytion, Hesperus IV, Thetis Prime, dozens of others—all obeyed him. All playing the same symphony: the Tenth. One movement was still missing. He possessed the finale, the middle. He just needed the beginning. The overture crafted to aid humanity, help it rise above its imperfections.

Now he would be forced to destroy that dream.

Enraged, Trestan blew Beethoven's home apart as he shifted once again in space-time. He rocketed through eras, a blazing entity bent on destruction, an arrow fired by Paris at the Scaen Gate where humanity desperately knocked to gain entrance.

A dulcet voice vibrated across the streams. Trestan homed in on it.

"You are a performer?" he asked Ulrika, who stood before him with hands on hips, her smile an oasis in the desert.

"We are all performers." Ulrika offered him a hand up the dune. "Some of us more than others."

MOVEMENT IV

12.

Presto Furioso in E major, Opus 31
January 27th, 1945
Auschwitz-Birkenau

Soviet troops cantered through the wooden gate on ponies. They stared with simple empathy at thousands of faces behind the barbed wire, many of them children. The prisoners' filthy striped uniforms contrasted the fresh snow around them.

Trestan realized he held a Luger pistol, while wearing a Nazi officer's uniform.

[322nd Rifle Division, Red Army. Threat level: 3.]

Upon seeing him, the Soviets aimed their guns. Trestan dropped the pistol and raised his hands. Some of them muttered to each other, then cocked their rifles.

"Where is she, Maryshka?" Trestan called. He didn't have time to worry if they were surprised that he spoke Russian.

One of the ponies galloped up to him. Maryshka leaned back in the saddle and unwrapped a scarf from around his face. "I thought all the scum had fled west."

"Or into the future," Trestan said.

Maryshka nodded to one of his soldiers. "Secure this one. I will question him."

While a Soviet trussed Trestan's hands behind his back, Trestan shook his head. "You've played into *Armée de L'ombre's* hands. You helped them destroy *Gott Lied.*"

"As did you." Maryshka led the soldiers into the concentration camp. A detachment released and fed the prisoners, while another tended the wounded. Trestan forced himself not to flinch when the soldiers found over six hundred smoking corpses. Many soldiers gave him hateful glances. He was receiving hatred he'd not earned, nor deserved. He too had fought for honor. But, he too had betrayed his cause.

Once Maryshka and Trestan stood alone outside the gate, Trestan straightened.

"Where is she?"

Maryshka dismounted and removed his hat. Sweaty black hair proved a magnet for the drifting snowflakes. "She enabled all of this. You helped her."

"You know that is a lie." Trestan wasn't sure if that were true, but he was stalling. His implants detected slight vibrations nearby, though from what source, he wasn't sure.

"We are masters of lies…or, at least, we once were." Maryshka produced an oscillator from inside his coat. "Now we are the slaves of the lies told by others. Lies that span centuries, entire civilizations. What lie brought these people here, caused their captors to treat them so? What lies brought me here, riding a shabby Cossack mount?"

"The same lie that brought Ulrika here," Trestan said. "Help me stop it."

"You will tell me the same thing three months from now, when my soldiers storm the rubble barricades in Berlin." Maryshka smiled sadly. "You cannot help me stop it, even if you wanted to. But…I can stop you. You are the link in the stream, Desaix."

Maryshka drew his blade. The same cavalry saber he'd carried since Borodino.

"She's probably in another time by now, while you wasted this moment with me."

"No moment is wasted." Maryshka raised the saber. "Only savored."

Trestan didn't close his eyes or turn away. There was no malice in Maryshka's stare. Only duty. Snowflakes fluttered around the razor-sharp steel.

Ulrika stared out the window as snowflakes floated past. "Stop pretending that you are honorable. That you really are a knight in shining armor, come to rescue me. You cannot even save yourself."

[Temporal lagging detected.]

Trestan's tuner located the vibration. It was within the concentration camp.

Maryshka's jaw tightened. Trestan remained still.

The vibration's source lay in the pile of burnt bodies.

"Wait," Trestan murmured, cold dread clawing into his heart.

"I will find her," Maryshka said. "I will stop her from igniting this war."

"This war began before we were born," Trestan said.

Maryshka beckoned a soldier over and prodded Trestan with the saber. "Over there. You need to see what Beethoven's work has wrought."

As they neared the unholy pyre, something caught Trestan's eye. Scraps of scorched jumpsuit hanging off a petite, blackened frame.

Trestan lurched forward. "No, no—!"

A soldier rammed the butt of his rifle into Trestan's stomach. Sobbing, Trestan fell to his knees. He felt the faint remnants of Ulrika's vibration, slowly decaying with each ripple. Slower and more painful was the decay in his heart. Feeding entropy, that starving, selfish scavenger of reality.

"I am sorry for you'." Maryshka removed his furred hat. "Yet, now you see. Close your eyes, and I will send you to her with one strike. From one man of honor to another."

Trestan balled his fists. The cold air made his tears glacial streams.

The vibration's final ripples were familiar. Leading elsewhere.

"What is this place?"

Ulrika smiled. "They call it Serapis."

"Desaix, I feel what you're doing." Maryshka backed away. "Shoot him if he tries to run. I'll not have us falling prey to another ambush like that one two days ago."

"Serapis was the Greek god of resurrection and abundance," Haydn said. *"Only a fool would have christened that lifeless world as such."*

Trestan activated his tuner. While the soldiers fired at where he'd been kneeling, he zipped between the streams and reappeared outside the concentration camp.

"You'll not escape!" Maryshka appeared right beside him, swinging the saber.

Ducking, Trestan lost his footing in the sand. He tumbled down the dune.

They were on Serapis.

"Ulrika!" Trestan scrambled up and scanned the empty horizon.

Maryshka charged after him. "I will follow you to any era, any world!"

Trestan raised his left forearm, warding off a blow meant for his head. The saber sliced through his uniform sleeve, to the bone. Blood poured from the wound.

"You cannot outrun time," Maryshka said. "Now, die like a man."

The vibration he'd detected at Auschwitz rippled over Serapis. Stronger.

As Maryshka thrust the saber, Trestan shifted to another stream. Now they stood among the remains of Barclay's cavalry at Borodino, butchered by French artillery. Saber in hand, Trestan barely deflected Maryshka's continued assault. Atop shattered men and horses, they dueled. Soon, Trestan bled from many cuts, while his foe remained unhurt.

"Haven't you seen enough death?" Trestan asked, shifting in pursuit of Ulrika's vibration. The carnage of Borodino gave way to a wooded hillock where a crowd gathered. They wore dull, somber clothing, with lacey ruffs, high collars. All the women wore caps. Everyone stared up at a stout oak tree. A young woman swung from it.

Ulrika.

"So passes Bridget Bishop," a stern-faced minister said. "May the Lord have mercy on her soul."

"How...?" Trestan murmured.

[Salem Witch Trials, June 10th, 1692. Puritan civilians. Threat level: 1.]

She swayed back and forth, head tilted at an unnatural angle. The lack of fear in her dull stare took Trestan aback. She'd wanted to die.

Cold steel touched his neck. "You are the enabler of her suffering. If you cherish her, why continue this?" Maryshka asked.

A tremor came from Trestan's implanted tuner. Her vibration continued, like it had at Auschwitz. After each death, Ulrika returned to Serapis, the Chorale's gateway, where she was healed. Resurrected. Like him, she couldn't die, for her personal vibration remained constant.

"Is she mad?" Maryshka lowered his saber, his face ashen. "I cannot fathom ..."

"You look as if you've seen a ghost."

Maryshka didn't look at him.

No matter how many times he witnessed her demise, no matter that she returned to Serapis—Trestan couldn't forget her dead face. Perhaps she had dwelled outside of time too long, and sought a final end.

Space-time shifted again.

They stood outside a palatial, castle-like residence with a grand red roof. Green spring grass and buzzing bees would have given a peaceful ambience, save for the American soldiers approaching in jeeps. They didn't notice Trestan or Maryshka.

"Where?" Trestan whispered.

[Garmisch Estate, April 30th, 1945.]

Ulrika's vibration emanated from the home. They rushed inside.

An American lieutenant waited at the bottom of a staircase while a distinguished, elderly gentleman descended the steps. Though the soldier remained ignorant of their presence, the old man stared at them.

"I am Richard Strauss, the composer of *Rosenkavalier* and *Salome*," the man said.

The lieutenant nodded and hurried outside, telling his unit. Trestan neared the staircase and met Strauss's steady gaze.

"You are the Frenchman?" Strauss asked in a soft voice.

"I am."

Strauss drew a silver chime from his jacket. "She left this for you."

The vibration came from it. But instead of the original Jupiter and Saturn embossing, the chime bore the image of a different ringed planet. Reading the engraved musical notes, he recognized the opening bars of *Also sprach Zarathustra*.

"Himmler and his wretched Ahnenerbe," Strauss said. "Despite all Wagner and I did to conceal it from them, they still used metaphonics in this inhuman conflict. Don't let them further abuse what so many have died for."

Once Mozart's coughing subsided, Trestan pointed at Haydn. "Your Gott Lied gave metaphonics to the Third Reich. Not Ulrika. Not Wagner. Do you have any idea what horrors they will unleash upon the world?"

Haydn watched as Fouché prepared Mozart's final poison dose. "They will be defeated. Those horrors you speak of will make people turn to the Creator once again for guidance. Just as he remade the world with flood, Gott Lied and its progeny will remake it in holocaust. They will have help, from the Americans with their bomb—"

"You're a madman," Trestan said.

"All prophets are thus accused." Haydn smiled.

"What folly is this?" Maryshka pointed at the chime. "That is an unstable device."

"She's leaving a trail," Trestan said.

Shouts outside. Gunfire.

Maryshka drew a phase pistol. Strauss sighed deeply and closed his eyes.

Several skeletal, metallic figures charged across the lawn. Each brandished pulse cannons, rocket tubes. Phase shifters. Instead of the former model's blank face, these sported Beethoven's death visage, the ultimate mockery of the composer's final dream.

[*Armée de L'ombre Mécanique* infantry, Build 4.1. Threat level: 4.]

"Talleyrand sent them. They'll follow us." Trestan rang the chime and shifted to where the vibrations led. Strauss, the estate, the American G.I.s—all was replaced by the starship docked with Hesperus IV.

Trestan and Maryshka wore spacesuits, their magnetic soles anchored to the asteroid's causeway. The robots appeared from nothingness, fired their boosters, and darted toward the ship.

"Go." Maryshka fired his phase shifter. One robot blew apart.

"What?" Trestan said "There is no hope here, we must find—"

"The woman you love ... what she has done ... that has restored my hope." Maryshka blasted another robot. "Now go!"

"Why? What did you see in the streams?" Trestan reached for him, but Maryshka kicked him aside and threw away his own tuner. The device flew into the starry expanse.

"You see the fruits of your revolution, and that is all you can say?" Maryshka grinned, then mounted his pony and galloped from Auschwitz. The prisoners cheered.

"What did you see?" Trestan yelled.

The robots fired. Pulse rounds and rockets ripped the ship apart, tilted the asteroid. Maryshka kept firing. As Trestan shifted, he felt the Russian's vibration end abruptly, like a piano wire snapping.

Trestan secured the chime inside his jacket as he waded through the audience to his seat. The orchestra had just started the Fourth Movement of the Ninth. He spotted Ulrika—Henriette Sontag, in this era—on the stage alongside the other soprano, Caroline Unger. Ulrika wore a white gown and a pearl necklace; a chestnut-haired angel about to sing the master of metaphonics to rest. Beethoven himself conducted, but out of time, turning the music pages and gesturing with sharp, impatient movements. Often he jumped up and down, asking for more exuberant playing, or cringed, indicating softer notes. Trestan wondered if the composer worked on another level, and if it was Trestan and the audience who were truly deaf.

"We are here." Wagner spread his arms as the orchestra finished playing.

Trestan and Ulrika floated beside Wagner atop a green and white planetary ring. It encircled a yellow-brown gas giant that rotated thousands of miles below. They all wore a thick spacesuit, with delicate instruments affixed to each thrustpack. His instruments indicated the rings weren't composed of ice or rock, like most planetary rings.

The megaliths Wagner's gravitational anomaly had brought fell to the gas giant. Moments later, they vanished in fiery streaks.

"Where?" Trestan asked.

[Phaenna, Class I gas giant. Pleiades Cluster, 135 parsecs from Earth.]

He jetted thrust until he was parallel with the edge of the ring. It was a flat world all its own, thousands of miles wide. His gloved hands brushed its glass-like edge.

"You don't need to do this," Ulrika said over the helmet's radio.

He showed her the silver chime. "Yes I do."

"We all do." Eyes full of fire, Wagner gestured.

Trestan felt a vibration of tones. His tuner translated it as the opening notes to the Prelude theme from *Tristan und Isolde*.

"You old fool." Ulrika and Wagner shared a brief smile.

The small objects comprising the ring all turned in unison. With a scintillation of light, the ring's pattern changed as trillions of miniscule devices changed position. It took a few moments for Trestan's implants to detect and translate what they were.

They weren't ice or rocks. They were oscillators.

13.

Allegro Trionfante in F major, Opus 31
May 7th, 1824
Vienna

The performance of the Ninth reached a crescendo. It became more complex, louder, filling Theater am Kärntnertor with an energy few attendees could identify.

Clasping the chime, Trestan shared in the experience tenfold. Ulrika serenaded them with florid passages, adding to the overall vibration in spacetime. The audience sat on the edge of their seats. Beethoven flung his head back and pointed heavenward.

They were creating the very music of the spheres.

Vibrations from Wagner's opera spread through the planetary ring, and soon, the entire structure rippled and glimmered. It was an invisible shockwave of information, traversing the cosmos on a far grander scale than anything Trestan had experienced.

They had found the Chorale's ultimate musical instrument.

The shockwave spread. One moment Trestan and the planet Phaenna were there; the next, they were appeared in a different solar system. Now it had a brighter sun, different stars in the distance, and two moons orbiting it.

His mind numbed at such an achievement.

"It is almost complete," Wagner said.

The slightest tremor disturbed Trestan's tuner. Then another. Moments later, a cascade of vibrations passed through Trestan and the others, en route to the planetary ring. It was too much data for his implants to decode, much less classify. But snippets of consciousness whisked through his mind. Memories, emotions.

[Temporal gateway opened. Threat level: 5.]

As Trestan turned around, a host of starships zipped into existence. Robot sentinels flew at them, firing. Wagner was disintegrated by a pulse round, and the explosion flung Trestan and Ulrika through the void. He managed to grab her. Together they spiraled like fallen angels toward Phaenna's opaque atmosphere.

Part of her suit was ripped in the blast.

She met his eyes. "My life-support module—"

"Wait, I can enter a new stream—"

Ulrika jerked as the final breaths inside her helmet rushed into the void.

Trestan held her close. She kept her gaze on him, face reddening from holding her breath. He covered the hole where the module hose had connected. It was no use.

The orchestra and choir joined forces to proclaim Beethoven's Ninth Symphony to the ages. Oblivious to the robots storming down the aisles, the audience held their breath. Trestan drew forth the chime and the bloodied tuning fork.

"Ulrika!"

"Trestan, I…" Her lips turned blue. Eyes rolled back, then fluttered closed.

"Whom have you promised my head… Salome?" Trestan smiled.

They fell through a rift in the very fabric of time. Reality bent and wrinkled around them. It was as if the starfield were a piece of paper, crumpled in someone's fist. Rips appeared in it, and they rocketed through these into other universes.

"Why, the future." Ulrika grabbed his hand and they ran across the dunes.

A tremor disturbed Trestan's tuner; the same he and Maryshka had followed. It was Ulrika's vibration, continuing like it had at Auschwitz. Concentrating, he viewed it through multiple eras. In each one, Ulrika died in someone else's place. Usually women, but sometimes children. Perishing under the guillotine instead of Olympe de Gouges, or taking a 'witch's' place at the stake.

Entering the gas chamber at Treblinka, so a Jewish teenager wouldn't have to.

Afterward, Trestan forced himself to find her body among the cadavers. Face frozen in terror, bleeding ears, foam dripping from rigid lips. Holding her, he wept.

The life vibrations of each person thus saved was channeled elsewhere in the universe. Resonating through the fabric of reality, undying. After each death, Ulrika returned to Serapis, the Chorale's gateway, where she was healed. Resurrected. Like him, she couldn't die, for her personal vibration remained constant.

Holding her rigid form, Trestan watched as balls of hot gas birthed stars. Rubble that was billion-year old orphans of previous celestial demises gathered together into planets, into solar systems, into galaxies. Over it all he sensed a harmony deceptive in its simplicity. It spread faster as gravity accelerated across countless light years. Carrying with it infinite vibrations designating galaxies, suns, worlds. Thoughts.

It seemed so close, Trestan extended his hand. "It's beautiful, Ulrika."

His conscious throbbed with the latent power awaiting his command. Power that could save Ulrika. Grant him whatever—even whenever—he wished.

"Be cautious of what you select as your addiction. This vice knows no return." Berlioz nodded at Ulrika as she walked around the stone circle on Eurytion. "Cheating death is a drug all its own, and a harsher master than any despot."

"It's beautiful." He ran his gloved fingers over her faceplate.

The Tenth's formula allowed him to direct the vibrations, not simply pass between them. Not merely shift from stream to stream. Now he could manipulate them.

Trestan tugged at Ulrika's stream. Varying it, while lengthening his own.

"I told you…" he cupped her face. "We're in this together."

"Goddamn you," Ulrika breathed. *"I didn't want this…"*

He squirmed in reddish sand, spying the moons of Serapis high above. It was twilight, with the sun passing the horizon. He wore clothing from his own era.

Ulrika lay beside him, wearing the black mourning dress. She wasn't breathing.

"No." He shook her, lightly slapped her cheeks, then pressed on her chest.

The human heart ran on electricity and pulsation, the vibrations of pumped blood and muscles. It was a biological engine, and like all engines, it could be restarted if all the components were extant. She had plasma, whole tissue and organs, finally had oxygen…

He kept pressing on her chest. She wasn't responding.

Haydn snorted. "You are beyond pity. Beyond hope, were it my say!"

"That is the true spirit of the Revolution," Trestan said. "To overthrow those who would cast us into Hell. To make Heaven for ourselves."

Haydn swung the wand at Trestan. Trestan caught it.

A metal cylinder lay in Trestan's grasp. Hollow, with a sheaf of paper inside. The ramifications of what he now held made Trestan shudder. His trembling fingers barely retrieved the costly prize inside.

It was the final fragment of Beethoven's Tenth Symphony. The overture.

"We did it." He cradled Ulrika's head in his lap. "Look, we…"

She vanished.

"You see?" Haydn laughed. "You are not gods. No more than the genius in this grave." He kicked pebbles into an open pit, where several wrapped corpses lay.

One of them was Mozart's.

Heavy steps crunched over the sand. Trestan sensed their vibrations disturbing the time stream, but he kept staring at his empty lap.

Scores of robotic soldiers surrounded him, aiming phase pistols and pulse cannons. They wore a new insignia: the fleur-de-lis, crowned with a ring of planets.

Talleyrand walked from among the robots. "Congratulations. You have performed remarkably in service of the Revolution. You shall be regaled by future generations as the one who sacrificed himself for the greater good. Now, give me that piece of manuscript. It has been too long since we've heard new music from the master."

"You killed her." Trestan slowly stood.

"Me?" Talleyrand shook his head. "No, you lovesick fool. She nearly delivered the Tenth to our enemies, but you stopped her. You saved us all."

"Enemies?" Trestan glowered. "The Third Reich and *Gott Lied* are destroyed. The Chorale and Maryshka Ulyanov, slain."

"True," Talleyrand said. "But she wasn't working for any of them. Or for me, ultimately, though she played her scheme. No, Ulrika served that primitive constituency that always raises its head at the worst of times."

"Who?" Trestan asked.

Talleyrand sniffed. "Humanity, of course. Now, surrender the fragment."

"The voice of the Creator cannot be understood, much less utilized, for mortal gain," Haydn said. "And now you have reaped what you have sewn. You might as well throw her in as well. Then, yourself." He indicated the open pit.

Inside lay Berlioz, Fouché, Maryshka, Wagner, and others that had died between the vibrations of time. Crows cawed from a dead tree overlooking the cemetery.

"You're wrong." Trestan clutched Ulrika's limp body.

Haydn smiled. "Unlike you, Frenchman, I am willing to accept what the Creator has in store for me. I willingly receive whatever punishment he has for me abusing the vibrations of time. It was necessary, to protect them from men like you." He removed his head and collapsed into the pit.

"No," Trestan said. "It is meant for all."

Talleyrand laughed. "You think anyone else, those ignorant of metaphonics, will ever be able to comprehend such power? Who but us deserves it? Who do you think Beethoven, and all those who came before him, made this for?"

"It is for a future humanity. One who will understand it. A future humanity that you'll not reach with your schemes."

The 'Ode to Joy' moment came. The crowd leaned forward, focused on the music, drawn to it as if physically pulled to the stage. Ulrika sang, her sweet, melodic voice creating a large vibration. It spread far beyond the venue; Trestan felt certain it was being played in all those empty orchestra pits across the Chorale's worlds. Forming an unbroken chain of harmony across the universe.

Talleyrand gave Trestan the coldest glare. "Cease this sedition. I can make you endure her death a million times, and in as many ways."

"I know all about death."

"Then enlighten us." Talleyrand smirked.

They shifted to the music parlor at Château de Valençay. Men in Imperial Guard uniforms held eagle banners from Napoleon's *Grande Armée.* Members of *Armée de L'ombre* languished on couches, wearing Beethoven's death mask.

One by one they removed the disguise, beaming at him. Once again he wore the old Imperial uniform. The saber at his side was Maryshka's.

Robots guarded the exits while maids served Chardonnay in chilled goblets. Talleyrand, ever the politico, meandered through the crowd, shaking hands. Finally, he stopped before Trestan and smiled. "Now, my good man. Reveal what you have learned."

Everyone raised tuning forks, oscillators, chimes, resonators. Waiting.

The Ninth's final notes blasted through Trestan's consciousness, for underlying its ending was the Tenth's beginning. It vibrated through his being, outward through space and time. Trestan stood with the rest of the audience and applauded, but his fanfare celebrated far more than the performance he'd just sat through. It was for the performance of an eternity.

Trestan slammed the bloody tuning fork into the silver chime. The resulting vibration rebounded off the other devices in the parlor, flinging their owners to the floor. A ripple of metaphonic force washed over them like a psychic earthquake. Trestan focused it, multiplied it. Their devices shattered. The robots exploded.

"Stop!" Talleyrand shouted. "There is no return! We'll all be trapped!"

Other worlds, other epochs shifted around them. Vienna 1827, Acre 1291, Proxima Centauri, Berlin 1945, the Cretaceous, Babylon 326 B.C., Thetis Prime. Gravity warped the time streams. With each shift, more of *Armée de L'ombre* were scattered without means to return. It took all his concentration not to join them.

"You will die here, damn you!" Talleyrand screamed, clinging to a piano. "You cannot control such forces, not even Beethoven could!"

"I have died a hundred times," Trestan said. "I will die many thousands more."

"Why?" Talleyrand cried. "Think of what you are doing!"

"The revolution is dead," Trestan said. "Long live the Revolution."

With a shriek, Talleyrand disappeared into the vastness above Hesperus IV.

Trestan fell to his knees as the building around him was torn apart in the gravitational maelstrom. Pieces of flesh ripped off his body. The tuner in his chest cracked and went dead just as he toppled down a sand dune.

Scraps of Imperial eagles lay at his feet, smoldering.

"Quintilius Varus … give me back my legions," he whispered.

Trestan watched as Ulrika was aided off the stage by adoring fans. A young, portly gentleman rose from his seat and grinned at Trestan.

"Such a wondrous performance." The gentleman sighed deep, as if inhaling air for the first time. "It is certainly one for the ages."

"Yes," Trestan said. "Most certainly, Herr…?"

"Schubert." He shook Trestan's hand. "Franz Schubert. I bid you good night, sir, and safe travels." He smiled again.

"And to you as well." Trestan frowned at the crowd as Ulrika left the theatre.

"You had best hurry. That songbird might fly away." Schubert chuckled.

Trestan grinned and hurried after her.

But once he reached the lobby, Ulrika was already gone. A mob of well-wishers and fans gathered round Beethoven. The festive, joyous feeling in the air permeated Trestan's being, but his chest hurt. He ran backstage and checked each dressing room, he inquired of the stagehands. He even checked the alleyway outside.

Henriette Sontag—Ulrika—was gone.

Trestan lay beside the stone columns, staring at Serapis's horizon with apathy. Though the planet's healing default mended his wounds, doubts gnawed at him. He'd never know if he saved humanity, nor if another metaphonics user would take advantage of such knowledge. Talleyrand had been right about one thing.

There was no way he could return to his time, his world.

Wetting his lips, Trestan recalled the piece Berlioz played on the guitar. Recalled dancing. He whistled the melody, helping the memory come alive, if only for a moment.

Trestan clasped her hand and led her into a dance. Ulrika took to the movement as naturally as a bird to flight. They capered round the parlor, round the Arc de Triomphe, round the cosmos itself, eyes locked as the vibration between them continued.

Mouth dry, he broke off whistling and coughed.

"Music is useless unless it is heard," Ulrika said.

Trestan turned. She stood between the columns, holding her oscillator. Even without an implanted tuner, he sensed her unique vibration—no longer sustained, no longer a stranger out of time. She wore blue silks, hair blowing in the wind.

"Exactly." He slowly stood.

Grinning, Ulrika grabbed his hand and they ran across the next dune.

ABOUT THE AUTHOR

Tony Peak is an Active Member of SFWA and an Affiliate Member of HWA. He is represented by Ethan Ellenberg of the Ethan Ellenberg Literary Agency. His debut novel INHERIT THE STARS was published by Penguin Random House in November 2015. His interests include progressive thinking, transhumanism, and planetary exploration. Residing in southwest Virginia, he has a wonderful view of New River.

ABOUT THE PUBLISHER

This book is published on behalf of the author by the Ethan Ellenberg Literary Agency.
https://ethanellenberg.com
Email: agent@ethanellenberg.com